Creative
Girls Club®

Mystery Book

Hidden in Plain Sight

By Ellie McDonald

Illustrations by John C. Ward

Annie's Attic®

Dedicated to all girls
who have a creative spark
and love a good mystery!

Lily

Hi, I'm Lily Matthews. I'm twelve years old and will be in the seventh grade. Five of my very best friends, all girls, have a club. I'm the lifetime president. My mom says I'm a natural leader, though I have led my friends into one or two adventures that she doesn't know about. Ahem. On the quieter side, I love crafts and keep my friends stocked with friendship bracelets. Not to mention cool club T-shirts with more starry glitter than a clear summer night in the little town where we live: Summary, Indiana. When my friends need help picking paint for their rooms, or want to know the latest in bulletin board fashion, I'm there! Actually, I painted stripes on my bedroom walls. Three colors. Pink, purple, and green. It took forever, but who cares? It's totally gorgeous. And when my friends need a fashion Band-Aid, they call Dr. Lily. If I don't know, I ask my big sister, Eileen, who knows everything. If you don't believe me, just ask her. I live with my mom, who is an accountant, and Eileen. Like them, I'm pretty tall and kind of lanky with long wavy, light brown hair and green eyes. When we go shopping together, people say we all three look like sisters—which makes my mom smile.

Sarah

Hi! I'm Sarah Carson, a member of the club. My family lives on an old estate that has a carriage house where they used to keep horses. Our club cleared out the tack room where they once stored the horses' equipment, and we use it for our meetings. I love to write and have had one story published in a magazine. And I'm the club poet! And the secretary. My dad works in sales and Mom is a homemaker. I have six brothers and sisters. I was born fourth, so I'm just in the middle. Sometimes I grab a book and climb out my bedroom window onto the roof just to get away from everybody. So far, nobody has found my secret place. When they ask where I've been, I say, "In another world." Which is true when I have a good book! My brothers say I'm vertically challenged—meaning I'm kind of short. Also, I'm just a bit chubby. You know. Leftover baby fat. I have blue eyes and sandy red hair, which my mother insists on cutting herself to save money. Yikes! Oh, I'm ten and will be in the fifth grade.

AnaMaria

Hola. I'm AnaMaria Torres, also a member of the club. I'm twelve and will be in the seventh grade. I'm the club artist, I guess. When I have extra time, I draw and paint. At school I helped with the painting of a mural, and in art class I learned to cast a figure of Shakespeare's head. I've worked and worked to make my small bedroom just as I like it. Our family is Hispanic, second-generation American, since my grandpa came from Mexico. Dad teaches and coaches at the Summary high school. Mom is a nurse. I have one little brother, Carlos. He's five and the uncrowned king of our family. I take care of him a lot, but this summer my mom has more time than usual. I'm not tall and not short either. I have dark, straight, shiny hair which—just between you and me—I'm wickedly proud of, and I spend part of my allowance to keep it perfectly shaped—long around my face and short in back. I have dark eyes and a pug nose that my dad says is cute. **Not.**

Kate

Hi! I'm Kate Waters, another club member. I'm eleven and will be in the sixth grade. I read a lot, love foreign languages, and even work with codes. WKLVPHVVDJHLVWRSVHFUHW. Got that? It says THISMESSAGEISTOPSECRET in Caesar Cipher. I'll tell you all about it someday. My friends say I'm a "brain," but they mean it kindly. They say things like, "Hey, brainiac! Who was Einstein?" and I can tell them he was a **real** brain. Our family is African-American. I'm the only child. My dad teaches languages at the local college and my mom travels a lot in her business. They're divorced, which is really sad. Dad and I live in a cozy condominium that is about overrun with books. We also have a nifty computer that I can use for research.

Elizabeth

Have you seen my lime green sunglasses that match my sparkly sequin top? Ah, here they are! Hello! I'm Elizabeth Anderson, age twelve, seventh grade, and I loathe meeting people for the first time without my sunglasses on. My mother is the same way—though I hardly ever see her. She was first-runner-up in the Miss World contest, and my dad says now she just runs around the world. Ha, ha. He should talk. This week he's in Egypt. Africa? Someplace. When he comes home, he'll bring me wonderful stuff. The best thing he brought me from his last trip was Trudy. Yes, a living, breathing, totally warm person. She's our housekeeper now and stays here with me. She's a fab cook. Today we're going to make a Viennese strudel. One last thing. Did you know you can eat flowers? Not a lot of people know that. That's why I'm growing this big bed of Creamsicle nasturtiums out by the pool. I love to grow things. Trudy and I put the nasturtiums in salad—makes it beautiful and spicy. Oh yeah . . . and I grow these blue dessert flowers too. But I'll have to tell you about those later. Actually, I'll have to tell you about my whole garden later. I have a little pot of bachelor buttons, daisies, and pink zinnias on my dresser. And I grew them. Imagine that!

Alex

Hi. I'm Alex James, last—but not least—of the club members. I love competition and have some trophies and ribbons for voice, clarinet, softball, track, basketball, and stuff. I tend to get a bit reckless sometimes. Once I jumped out of a barn loft and **didn't** land on a horse. My friends say I watch too many action movies. Maybe. I'd love to start taking lessons at Monique's Dance Salon. A leotard might be more fun than a softball jersey. Then I could sing and dance—which might come in handy sometime. My mom teaches gym at the high school and my dad is a diesel mechanic who sings country music when he works. Even though I'm only eleven and in sixth grade, I'm the tallest girl in the club and have long legs. I can never find jeans that fit. My hair is short and blond; my eyes are blue. Mom says my face is square and pretty. Of course, I'm far too modest to agree to that!

Chapter 1

June was perfect for doing nothing in Summary, Indiana.

Lily rocked back and forth on the front porch swing, rolling her toes against the cool gray floor. The swing said *creak* when she rocked forward and *crack* when she rocked back. It made a friendly sound—a sound so soothing and happy that Lily felt like singing. So she did.

> *"Oh, the moonlight's fair tonight along the Wabash,*
> *From the fields there comes the breath of new-mown hay."*

She couldn't quite come up with the next line, though she knew it. As she hesitated, a mature soprano prompted her from the sidewalk.

"Through the sycamores the candle lights are gleaming,
On the banks of the Wabash, far away."

"Thanks!" Lily said. She couldn't make out any details about the woman because she stood exactly against the ten o'clock sun as it popped over the Nelsons' house across the street. But whoever she was, she was tall, and she wore a large sun hat that covered her hair and hid her expression.

"You have a beautiful voice," Lily told the woman. "And you know all the words, too."

The woman laughed. "Well, maybe not all of them. But thanks for the compliment. Lovely day," she said. "I think I—"

The telephone rang inside the house. Lily's mother was at the office and her older sister had worked late the night before.

"Sorry," Lily said, jumping up. "The phone!"

By the time Lily stepped back outside with the telephone cradled between her chin and shoulder, the woman was strolling down the sidewalk. She moved as if she too thought that June was perfect for doing nothing.

"Lily!" Sarah gasped on the other end of the line. "Oh, Lily, the most awful thing has happened ..."

Chapter 2

By two o'clock, everybody had assembled for a special crisis meeting.

"The meeting will come to order," Lily said.

Lily counted the club members off in her head. Sarah, Kate, Elizabeth, Alex, AnaMaria, and herself, Lily, lifetime president of the Silly Stuff Club.

All present.

The Silly Stuff Club was a group of friends who collected things like old phonograph records, though they didn't have a machine to play them on. They met weekly to have their show-and-tell for girls only.

They met in the Carsons' carriage house—which led Lily to today's emergency meeting agenda. Sarah's family was moving to Chattanooga. So by the end of summer, the club would be without Sarah and minus one clubhouse.

"But your parents can't move away just … just like that," AnaMaria said, snapping her fingers, ignoring Lily's call to order.

Lily flopped down on a trunk, sending up a small puff of dust. It was so hot in the Carsons' carriage house that her palms stung with sweat. Why hadn't she put her hair up in a ponytail this morning? It was sticking to her neck.

"Just tell your daddy you won't go to Chattanooga." Elizabeth shrugged a shoulder. Today Elizabeth wore a sequined turbanlike thing on her hair. And her lime green sunglasses perfectly matched her sandals. "Slam your door and refuse to come out until he swears on his grandmother's grave not to drag you off to Chattanooga."

That might work in Elizabeth's house, but Lily doubted that it would at the Carsons'. She glanced out the dusty cracked window of the carriage house. Three of Sarah's brothers kicked a soccer ball around. Two of her little sisters drew an enormous rainbow with sidewalk chalk in front of the garage. And beside them, Sarah's older sister banged a tennis ball off the garage door.

"My parents don't notice anything less than a Category 4 hurricane," Sarah said. "I'm not an only child like you."

"Pooh," Elizabeth said, pursing her lips. "Don't you know how to pitch a hissy? Throw a window-rattling, door-slamming, refuse-to-come-out-of-your-room-for-three-days tantrum?"

Sarah shook her head.

Lily sighed. It probably was hopeless. In her experience, parents did what parents did.

Lily's five friends had been in the Silly Stuff Club

with her since third grade. Today they stood, squatted and sprawled among the trunks, boxes and chairs that they'd dragged into the small carriage house over the past three years.

"What will we do with all our stuff?" Lily sighed, spreading her arms to include everything.

"Isn't your sister going away to college?" Alex asked. "Maybe we could move it into her room."

"And die," Lily assured them.

"Well we can't move it to our place," Kate announced. "Dad and I live in a town house. And there's barely room for three tiny tetras and two black mollies. Where would we put something like a dressmaker's dummy?" She pointed to the big body-shaped wire thing. At first the girls had thought that it was underwear for a suit of armor, until Kate set them straight.

"A month ago maybe we could have moved it above our garage," AnaMaria said. "But did I tell you that my grandmother is coming from Mexico to live with us? My father is fixing her an apartment up there. I'm helping decorate it!"

"It won't fit in our place," Alex said, folding her size extra-long legs to her chest and hugging them. "My mom made me clean out a bunch of soccer equipment and softball and basketball stuff. She said the house is about to burst."

Their eyes settled on Elizabeth. She made a dramatic Elizabeth gesture, holding them off with rigid arms. "Honestly, no," she said. "My folks would never go for it. Not here. Maybe at our farm in Vermont. It has outbuildings. But here …" She shook her head, making the sequins sparkle. "Nix and double nix."

No.

So what were they going to do?

Lily picked up a ratty red canvas high-top shoe. It was a perfect example of the kind of stuff they needed to find a home for. She herself had brought the shoe to the Silly Stuff Club, and the girls had gone nearly comatose with laughter. Long ago, some boy had inked on the sole: "I LOVE MELVA WINSTON'S HOG."

But a little research (Lily had asked Grandpa Max one night at supper) showed that the shoe had been worn for playing basketball. The "hog" referred to a big motorcycle. And Melva Winston had blasted out of town on her Harley nearly half a century ago, leaving broken hearts in the exhaust.

"Melva Winston." Lily spoke aloud without really meaning to.

"What?" Kate asked, her dark eyes curious.

"Melva Winston rode out of town on her motorcycle and never came back." Lily waggled the shoe at her friends. "Maybe there's an answer to our problem here."

"In that nasty old shoe?" Elizabeth's right eyebrow arched over her lime green sunglasses.

"The abandoned estate down at the end of this road is called the old Winston estate." Lily touched her temple. "Nobody has seen or heard from Melva Winston in almost half a century, and she was the heiress."

"The what?" asked AnaMaria.

"She inherited everything! She gets to keep all the family's money and stuff."

Lily watched her presidential thought take hold in her friends' minds. Probably nobody would be using the old Winston estate.

AnaMaria nodded. "I'll bet that old place has buildings like this one! Not that you can actually see anything—"

"Yeah, all you can see sticking up over that brick wall is a bunch of chimneys," Alex interrupted. "There must be ten of them. That place is huge."

"My mom says that if any of us go near it, we're grounded 'til we're old enough to vote," Sarah mumbled, trying to smooth her sandy red hair. "Mom gave us haircuts last night, and while she was doing mine, Nicky shoved a bean up his nose. Tell me the truth," she said, turning her head from side to side. "How bad does it look?"

Lily couldn't think of anything presidential to say. So she was glad when Elizabeth piped up with a suggestion to take Sarah to her hair stylist. "She charges heaps. But, oh well," Elizabeth sighed, "what are friends for, huh? We can't go around looking like somebody has been hacking at us with kindergarten scissors."

"Back to the old Winston estate," Lily reminded them.

"That gate has more 'KEEP OUT' signs than my brother's bedroom door," AnaMaria said. "We couldn't possibly move the club there." She shook her head, making her shiny dark hair swing around her cheeks.

"We could just go look at it," Alex argued. She bounced on her feet as if somebody had tossed her a soccer ball and pointed her toward the goal. "Just for fun."

Had Alex's legs really grown longer during this meeting? Or was it Lily's imagination?

"It wouldn't hurt to look. Think of the privacy we'd have there," Elizabeth said.

"Think of the trespassing we'd do there," Kate reminded them.

"It could be really, really dangerous," Sarah argued. "We don't know what's on the other side of the wall. Plus," she concluded, "my mom says I can't."

"But you're moving away," Elizabeth pointed out.

Sarah's eyes shone with tears as her mouth dropped open.

"Oh I didn't mean it like that," Elizabeth said, jumping up and running to hug Sarah.

Lily could tell by the way they all gathered around Sarah that the real problem was sinking in. Sarah would be the first member of their club, ever, to move away. If she was gone, who would write poems for their birthdays? And little club essays to celebrate special occasions?

Sarah tugged nervously on her friendship bracelet, which Lily had personally knotted for her. Sarah's eyes moved from girl to girl. "Mom says I'll make new friends. But I don't want new friends," she said, starting to cry. "I just want my old ones."

Everything would be different without Sarah.

And it hit Lily for the first time that the Silly Stuff Club wouldn't really last forever, like their bylaws said. And she wouldn't really be president for life. "Do I hear a motion that this meeting is adjourned?" she asked, wiping sweat and tears from her face.

Kate raised one finger.

"It'll be OK, honestly ..." the girls babbled, huddled around Sarah. "... e-mail you every day ... Chattanooga can't be that far ... visit ... never forget you ... not moving until the end of summer anyway ... have two whole months ..."

"A second?" Lily asked.

Elizabeth raised two fingers.

"Meeting adjourned," Lily sighed. She tapped the windowsill lightly with the old red canvas high-top.

Elizabeth said, "Let's go to Eli's and get stuffed on cheesecake. Then we'll all feel better. C'mon. My treat."

Lily, as president, carried the key. As she pulled the door closed behind her, she glanced at their huge collection of stuff. Did she really still care about the old hand-cut square nails that Alex had found somewhere? (Square nails were very silly, everybody agreed on that.) Did she care about the mouse-chewed autograph book with the pages of comic verse?

"Cows love corn, pigs love squash,
I love you, I do, by gosh."

And Lily's personal favorite:

"The sea is wide, the ocean is deep,
My love for you is as big as a sheep!"

Did she care about the lady's hat with a plastic canary on top that you could blow like a whistle?

Who had brought the hat to the Silly Stuff Club? If they

had to disband, would everybody remember what belonged to whom?

Disband? How could she even think of such a thing?

But some of the stuff—the actual stuff—was starting to seem ... well, kind of silly.

And hardly anybody brought new stuff anymore. They mainly just talked and painted each others' toenails.

Chapter 3

At Eli's sidewalk cafe, Lily snagged a raspberry sparkling water. Then she dropped into one of the chairs around a circular table shaded by a big green umbrella.

The patio was empty except for a woman sipping a tall, coffee-colored drink. The woman's long, thick hair was parted down the middle. Half was a silver gray that went with her aging face. The other half was the color of strawberry ice cream. It was actually very ... pink.

Lily could tell that AnaMaria, Kate and Alex had noticed her, too, by the way they carefully didn't stare.

"Wow," Sarah whispered, sitting down with her back to the woman. "Did you ever see such hair? Such a braid? It looks like a huge snake lying over her shoulder."

The thick twist of silver and strawberry pink did look like a fanciful boa constrictor. Just exactly.

"Amazing," AnaMaria breathed.

Elizabeth came with the tray and set out six forks, a stack of napkins, and three big pieces of cheesecake, all with different toppings.

"Don't stare, ladies," she murmured under her breath. Then more loudly, she said, "Pig out, girlfriends. Be hogs."

And they laughed, glancing at Lily.

Yeah, yeah. Her idea about the old Winston place was not all that stupid.

Lily chugged half her sparkling water before she twisted her hair up into a ponytail. "Anybody got a scrunchie? It's so hot."

Elizabeth dug in her purse, which, all the girls knew, had come from Tuscany where she and her family rented a villa every March. "Which one would you like?" she asked, pulling out three.

Lily chose a sage colored one with a gold thread spun through it and wrapped it around her hair.

"Pretty," Elizabeth said, cocking her head at Lily's new look. "Keep it. I have a zillion."

"Thanks, Liz," Lily said, glad for the breeze on her neck.

Elizabeth leaned toward the center of the table. She spoke so softly her lips barely moved. "Did you notice the tattoo when you walked by?"

Everybody's head came toward Elizabeth's until the girls' faces were only inches apart.

"On a woman her age?" Sarah breathed.

"Well, it's discreet," Elizabeth whispered, showing off a new word. "Just a tiny white rabbit on her left shoulder.

Hardly bigger than a freckle, really. I saw it when I went to get the napkins."

"She's probably visiting from California," Alex whispered. "Or some other exotic place."

"Look," Sarah said. "Do you suppose that's her boyfriend?"

A man about the same age in suspenders, his hair gray, greeted the woman with a smile. He said a few words that the girls couldn't make out.

"That's Les Dudley," Elizabeth told them. "He built some cabinetry for my mom's closet, and did some wiring for the dining area around the pool."

The girls gossiped for a while. They wondered where the strange woman might have come from. And was Les Dudley her beau, or was he just getting carpenter's specs?

But before long, Sarah sighed and stood up. "I gotta go. It's my turn to help fix supper tonight."

"And I'm supposed to walk my little brother to piano lessons at four thirty." AnaMaria stood up too. "Next week at the carriage house?"

"Next week," several voices said.

"Or sooner," Lily reminded them. "If anybody gets any good ideas about where we can move our stuff, call or e-mail, OK?"

On the way out, Lily tried to get a peek of the tattoo on the woman's shoulder, but just then the woman turned away.

Chapter 4

Alex, Kate, and Elizabeth lived in the same direction as Lily. So they walked down Market Street together, past Haas' Bakery, Dave's Variety Store, Westie's Shoe Emporium, and the law offices of Tuppin, Pierce, and Hardley. A tall man with a noticeably fish-shaped face ambled out the door. He climbed into a red BMW parked in a no-parking space.

"That's Mr. Tuppin," Elizabeth said. "My dad knows him. Did you know they call him 'Snapper'?"

"That can't be his real name," Kate said. "Who would name their kid 'Snapper Tuppin'? It's probably 'Henry' or something."

Elizabeth shrugged. "My dad calls him 'Snapper.'"

At Seventh Street, Elizabeth turned left. "Bye-bye," she said, and added a beauty-queen wave. "See you later."

"So should we go explore the old Winston place?" Alex

asked. Her blue eyes sparkled with the idea of adventure.

"Trust me, that is seriously not a good idea," Kate said. "Don't you remember hearing about the man who drowned in an abandoned well on the property?"

"That's ancient history," Alex scoffed.

"Still. It happened."

"Yes, yes, it happened. But it happened at night, right?" Alex looked to Lily for support.

"Probably," Lily said, not knowing for sure. It had been a long time ago. Maybe twenty years. Long before they were born.

"So we could go during the day," Alex said. "The three of us. And we could take a rope in case one of us fell down a well," she said, speaking directly to Kate. "And we could take an emergency flare."

"And we could take a twelve-foot ladder," Kate said. "So we can get over the wall."

Alex ignored Kate's sarcasm. "Not necessary. We're all tall. I'm strong. And Kate, you're so skinny you weigh hardly anything. I think we can help each other scramble over the wall."

"You've seen too many action movies," Kate complained.

"Oh, come on," Alex argued. "What harm will it do to just go look at the place? We'll just look. I promise. If it gets dangerous or scary … well, we can turn back anytime."

"And then we can make an informed report at the next meeting," Lily said, thinking presidentially. "Either the plan will have possibilities or … it won't."

"Right," Alex said cheerfully. "If the old Winston estate doesn't work out, we can sell all our silly stuff at a garage sale and disband."

Lily and Kate stared at her. They couldn't disband.

The look on Alex's face said she knew she had them.

"All right." Kate sighed. "When?"

"Tomorrow morning, ten thirty. Meet at the gazebo. I'll bring everything."

Alex turned right at Seventh Street. She leapt onto the retaining wall behind the Fast Stop, did a little dance, and turned to wave at them.

Lily and Kate waved back.

"Want to come in and help me organize my French notes?" Kate said when they got to her house.

Kate was insanely organized. Her tri-folded T-shirts rose in neat columns on tidy shelves. Her CDs marched down the rack alphabetically. So of course Kate would organize her French notes ... whatever *they* were.

"French notes?" Lily asked.

"Yeah, my dad and I are taking conversational French at the community center. Class started last night. Each night somebody brings *potage*, which means 'soup,'" she said, glancing at Lily. "Somebody else brings *pain*, which is 'bread,' and somebody else brings *dessert*."

"Which means 'dessert,'" Lily concluded, glad she knew at least one word of French.

"Exactly." Kate said. "And maybe organizing French notes is a one-person job," she decided, turning up her walk. "It might be kind of boring to another person."

"Probably not boring," Lily said. "But I need to get home anyway. So I'll see you tomorrow."

"At the gazebo," Kate agreed. "Tomorrow."

At her own house, Lily sat in the porch swing for a while, rocking back and forth. She listened to her sister inside talking to somebody on the phone. The key to the Carsons' carriage house made a bulge in her pocket. She took it out and studied it. Whatever would they do if they couldn't find a new clubhouse?

Chapter 5

The next morning, Lily got to the gazebo first. But soon she saw Alex and Kate striding toward her—Alex's long legs bare and muscular, Kate's dark-skinned and slim.

"Where's your flare gun? And the rope?" Lily asked.

Alex blew out her breath and shook her head. "If you were a grown-up—as in Sarah's mother—and saw three kids going down to the end of Summary Lane with ropes and a flare gun, what would you think?"

"That they were going to check out the old Winston place?" Kate volunteered.

"Exactly," Alex said. "It's daylight. We're together. We'll be careful."

Lily looked at Kate, who shrugged. They probably wouldn't be able to get over the wall anyway.

As they approached Eli's, Lily scanned the people

sipping morning coffee on the patio.

"Do you suppose the woman with the pink and silver hair will be back?" Kate asked, reading Lily's mind.

"Nah," Alex said. "I think she was just visiting. She's probably gone on to wherever by now."

"Maybe to the Sorbonne," Kate said. "She could be Parisian, you know. Don't you think she looked like she spoke French?"

"How does somebody look like they speak French?" Alex asked.

"Well," Kate said, "take that man there, for instance. The one with the dent in his chin, eating cherry cheesecake. He looks as if he speaks American English with a Texas accent." To prove her point, she nodded to him and called, "Hi!"

Lily elbowed her. "Don't speak to strangers!" she hissed under her breath.

The man had his mouth open to receive the bite of cheesecake dripping with cherry topping. He lowered the fork and stared at the three girls.

"Sorry," Kate called. "I thought you were Nancy's dad."

He stared at them harder as they passed.

"Who's Nancy?" Lily whispered.

Kate ignored her. "Sorry," Kate said again, over her shoulder.

"'S'all right, darlin'," the man finally called. "Anybody's mistake."

"See?" Kate whispered. "He dripped Texas talk."

"But that was too easy," Lily said. "He had on cowboy boots and faded jeans. The woman with the exotic hair had on ordinary clothes."

"But she stood out," Kate said. "Like Parisian women do. You should see our French teacher. She's so elegant. And she's African American, like my family, but she lived in Paris for seven years. I think my dad should ask her to a movie."

They continued north a few blocks and turned onto Summary Lane.

"When we go past Sarah's, we had better look the other way," Alex advised. "We're on official club business, but still, we don't want her mom to spot us."

Nobody paid any attention as they hurried along in front of the Carsons' vast yard in the sunshine. They kept walking until they came to the very end of Summary Lane.

"Well, there it is," announced Alex.

They stood in front of the iron gates. Wild grapevines tangled through the bars with a thickness that said the gates hadn't been opened in forty years.

On top of the brick wall, a plastic grocery sack, caught in the barbed wire, stirred and snapped in the breeze.

"KEEP OUT." "NO TRESPASSING." "TRESPASSERS WILL BE PROSECUTED." "BEWARE OF DOG." "NO ADMITTANCE." "PRIVATE PROPERTY."

"I'll bet there's no dog," Alex said. "Not really."

Probably not. But Lily still felt in her bones that they should stop here, go no farther. "This is a bad idea, Alex," she said. "Maybe we can talk Elizabeth's family into letting us use their maid's quarters or something for our club."

"Then what would the maid use?" Alex asked. "The old

Winston place?" She began leading the way around the tall brick wall. "If we can find a spot where the barbed wire has fallen off the top, then I'm sure we can scramble over."

They walked on. Lily's ankles began to itch from the weeds. She clapped her hands at the gnats hovering around her face. Above the woods that stretched beyond the wall, a buzzard circled slowly in the hot summer sky.

Alex strode purposefully, watching the top of the wall for a break in the barbed wire. The sun glinted off her blond hair.

They'd worked their way around to the back of the property when Lily, whose neck was tired from looking up, noticed the door.

She grabbed Alex's shirt.

"What?"

Lily pointed.

There in the wall was a warped door built of vertical planks, faded with age. She would have missed it if she hadn't been smacking gnats at that precise moment. "It'll be bolted from the inside," Alex scoffed. "Just like the front gate."

"You're obsessed with going over that wall, girl," Kate said as Lily pushed down on the rusted thumb latch.

It gave an inch.

And then, with a grating squeal of hinges that sounded like the world was tilting on its axis, it opened against her weight. Nobody could have been more surprised than she was.

Still, none of the girls went through.

A dribble of sweat rolled down Lily's spine. This was too easy.

"I'd guess that's not been used in about a hundred years," Kate finally said. "It's the gardener's gate. See, he'd haul his stuff out through that door and dump it behind the wall." And, to prove herself correct, she pointed to a weed-covered mound that they could barely make out.

"How do you know all that stuff?" Alex demanded.

Kate shrugged. "From reading historical novels. All the old estates had gardeners. And they had to get out the back some way with their wheelbarrows."

"Oh," Alex said. Then, after a moment, she reminded them, "I guess we can go in now."

But nobody stepped forward. Even Alex seemed to have lost her bravado.

"Madam President," Kate finally said quietly, "after you."

Lily took a breath. This had been her idea. It was that stupid old tennis shoe and the ridiculous message about Melva Winston's hog.

She sucked in her breath and squinted her eyes, braced for … what?

She stepped through the doorway.

In the enormous backyard, insects hummed. A meadowlark sang "Marie, pretty bird! Marie, pretty bird!" from its perch high on a chimney.

"Come on," Lily said, motioning to Kate and Alex. "It's OK."

The two girls were standing on the other side of the doorway, looking at her.

"Come on," Lily said. "It's just an old backyard."

That wasn't quite true. Most backyards didn't have small stone buildings totally overgrown with vines, or tumbled statues bleeding rust spots. Most backyards didn't have broad, moss-covered steps that went down a bank to ... nothing. Or a sprawling, scummy, shallow pond blanketed with dragonflies.

Kate screamed when something splashed into the pond.

"Just a frog," Lily said.

"How do you know?" Kate asked.

It was very quiet. But then again, they were enclosed by a twelve-foot-high brick wall. They could scream their heads off and nobody would hear them.

They picked their way through the grass, which was waist-high in places, toward the back porch.

"I think there's been a deer through here," Kate said. "Look how the weeds are mashed down."

As they expected, the heavy door—when they finally got to it—was locked. But Alex used the front of her shirt to rub a clean space on one of the windows. Then she bent down to look inside.

"What do you see?" Lily asked.

"Just a room. Like maybe a mudroom. There's a bench, and some pegs on the wall."

Kate went around the corner to the right and looked in another window. "Just the kitchen," she reported. "An old stove. Cupboards and shelves."

What had they expected? Shrouded furniture that scuttled around the room when nobody was looking? Suits of armor? Organs that wheezed and gasped when the moon was full?

At Lily's house, they kept a spare key on a string behind the mailbox. Didn't all houses have spare keys somewhere outside?

There was no mailbox by the back door, but a wooden storage box sat by the porch railing. Lily opened it.

A pair of old rubber boots. A filthy black umbrella in which dirt daubers had nested. A mouse-gnawed notebook. A rusted hammer. And … she knew it!

A key.

It slid in the keyhole and, with only a little forcing, turned. Lily tried the knob and leaned against the door.

"Hey!" she called, motioning to Kate and Alex. "We're in!"

"How did you do that?" Alex demanded.

"Always try the simplest solution first. There had to be a spare key, right?" She motioned to the open box. "In the bottom."

She dropped the key into her pocket with her key to the Silly Stuff clubhouse. Who knew? Maybe she now carried both the old key and the new key.

Chapter 6

The house seemed to have power of its own, the ability to pull them in and point the way. Lily had the sense that she knew exactly where she was going, although, in fact, she didn't have the least idea. There were so many doorways, hallways, stairways, closets, and rooms. … Would they be able to find their way back out?

Kate whispered, but even her whisper echoed in the vast, empty space. "Look how high the ceilings are!"

"Feel how cool it is," Lily said. The sweat on the backs of her itchy legs dried deliciously.

The house, as if it were a living guide, led them through the mudroom and the kitchen. In the next room, which looked like a huge walk-through closet, shelves ran up the walls to the ceiling and a ladder hung from rollers. Alex leapt onto it, making the wheels screech in their tracks.

"Shhhhhhhhh!" both Lily and Kate hissed. The sound seemed to roll through the house, going away and then coming back to them, sounding more human as it grew fainter.

"Sorry," Alex whispered.

The odd closet led them into the next room.

"Dining room," Lily said, pointing to the table—covered with dust, but big enough to seat everybody in the Silly Stuff Club and all their families, including Sarah's. They came to a large, open entryway.

"You could put our whole entire house in here," Lily whispered.

"Man, I see why they built a brick wall around this place," Alex said, pointing to the stained glass that ran two full stories behind the winding staircase.

"Where did these people get so much money?" Lily wondered aloud.

"Well, I did a little research last night," Kate confessed. "My dad and I stopped by the library on the way home from French class. The money came from pharmaceuticals."

"Pharmaceuticals?" Alex echoed. "What's that?"

"Drugs. Medicine," Kate answered. "See, a certain Dr. Winston, a few generations back, discovered some miracle cure for an equine disease."

"Equine?" Alex again.

"Horses," Kate explained. "Basically, Dr. Winston developed these really great horse pills. And that's how the family fortune was built. He went a little nuts, though, in the end. At least according to the local newspaper. Did strange things. Like trying to bury all the family silver under the gazebo in the city park. Putting barbed wire on top of the wall."

No matter how the Winstons had made their money, Lily had never seen anything quite as beautiful as the stained glass windows. Despite the years and years of dust, they gave the effect of being just barely under water on a sunny day. She could practically feel her legs and arms being tickled by the ripples of small fish and weeping willow branches.

She crossed the room and started up the winding staircase, following the magnetic pull of the pale green light. "Come on," Lily said to her friends.

The other girls followed.

On the second floor, Lily saw three sets of wide, carpeted corridors going out from the landing. Each corridor had a tall, arched window far away at the end.

"Just like a hotel," Alex murmured.

In the stillness, Lily could almost hear the voices of children and their nannies. She pulled herself away, leading the girls on up the next flight of stairs.

On the third floor, they peered down the narrow hallways. The light was much dimmer, the floors bare and streaked with dust.

"Servants' quarters," Kate said.

Lily nodded, imagining she heard the creak of the boards under the servants' feet.

"Shhhhhhhh," Alex breathed. "Listen."

Lily shivered. Could Kate hear them too?

"Mice," Kate announced. "In the walls."

Alex shuddered. "I hate mice!"

"So," Kate said, "are we at the top?"

Wouldn't there be an attic? Just as everybody had a spare key hidden somewhere, didn't everybody have an attic? Wouldn't a wonderful house like this, of all houses, have an attic?

"Let's look for the attic," Lily suggested.

And they found it. At the end of one of the halls was an open doorway to a narrow flight of stairs. Lily gazed up into the darkness.

"Well, shall we?" she asked, after a while.

"We could hold hands," Kate suggested. Then she added, "You know. Just for fun."

Lily clutched Kate's hand, and Kate grabbed Alex's.

"We could whistle," Kate suggested.

"Or we could just be really quiet," Alex said under her breath, "until we've checked things out."

Kate's palm felt cold and sweaty against Lily's.

The attic stretched far into the dimness. As Lily's eyes began to adjust, she saw small dormer windows leaking in tiny bits of light. Great brick pillars, which would be the house's many chimneys, thrust up through the space. Otherwise, the room seemed vastly and totally empty.

"Wow," Alex breathed.

"Yeah … wow," Kate whispered.

Lily had thought the attic would be full of stuff. Weren't all attics full of stuff? Stuff. Silly stuff. Were the other girls thinking the same thing?

"It could be wonderful for our club," Alex said, walking a few feet into the room.

"It's so clean," Kate marveled, walking a few feet farther. "No cobwebs. No bat doo."

Almost as if somebody had prepared it for them. Lily shivered, glancing over her shoulder. They couldn't actually see what was behind the brick pillars. Like the dark side of the moon … if you couldn't see it, how did you know what was there?

"Why isn't it hot?" Alex mused. "My grandma's attic is about two hundred degrees in the summer."

Lily had been wondering that too. The air in this attic was cool and still. A lot cooler than the Carsons' old carriage house.

"It must be the thick stone walls," Kate said. "And the tile roof. This house is built sort of like a castle."

"It could be a great place for a clubhouse," Lily decided aloud.

As her eyes adjusted to the dimness, she could make out spaces by the windows. They would be just right for rugs and folding chairs where they could have meetings or gab. Nobody would ever be able to hear a word they were saying.

"Nobody would find out our secrets up here," Alex said.

"And we could spread our silly stuff out, rather than having it crammed into the carriage house," Kate added.

It was just about perfect.

"AnaMaria could help us make it beautiful and cozy in no time," Alex said. "You know how she can do that. A striped rug here. A patch of paint there."

Lily squatted down by the nearest window and looked out. There was the Carsons' place to the south, looking surprisingly small from up here. There was Summary itself, hidden by trees except for the spire of the Methodist church. Lily had never felt so private. Nobody in the world, except her two friends, had any idea where she was.

"But we're still trespassers," Kate said.

"So?" Alex returned. "Who cares? I mean, nobody else is using it, and we're not going to hurt anything."

"But what would our parents say?" Lily asked.

"We don't tell them," Alex answered.

"How would we get all our stuff up here without anybody seeing?" Kate asked.

"Sneak it up at night?" Alex proposed.

But Lily could tell by the looks on the girls' faces that they knew it would be harder than it sounded. It would take incredibly good planning. Maybe they could tell everybody's parents that they were having a slumber party at Elizabeth's, and then tell Elizabeth's family that they were having a slumber party at Lily's. Something like that.

"The old slumber party trick," Alex proposed, reading her mind.

Kate and Lily nodded.

"But how would we actually move all our stuff?" Kate asked. "We'd look like an army of ants running up and down Summary Lane in the moonlight."

"Somebody would probably notice," Alex admitted.

"And we've got so much stuff," Kate sighed. "Think of hauling it down the road and up into this attic. I'd die of exhaustion."

Lily wanted to stomp her feet and yell, or "pitch a hissy,"

as Elizabeth would say. How could something so perfect be so impossible? She sighed. As president of Silly Stuff Club, she had to take charge. "The attic is great. But unfortunately," she pronounced, "it will never work."

"Don't be so sure," said a new voice.

Lily whirled around.

Chapter 7

Kate and Alex jumped away from the window, and Alex crouched down to spring. All three screamed.

Thoughts jumbled in Lily's head. Nobody would ever hear their screams. ... They should have looked behind all those chimneys. ... She should never have proposed this stupid idea. ... She had led her friends into ... what?

"Stay away from us," Alex commanded, her voice loud but unsteady. "We were just leaving."

The tall figure stepped closer to the girls, closer to the light.

"Stay away!" Alex shouted.

The woman squatted down so she was more or less level with Alex.

The sweat of pure panic began to dry on Lily's body as she recognized the woman from Eli's. The woman with the pink and silver hair. But it wasn't braided today. It sprang out in crazy, incredible amounts as if it had magical powers.

"Don't be frightened," the woman said, her voice even and warm. "I'm sorry I scared you. But I heard somebody in the house, and I was a bit scared myself. So I ran up here and hid." She laughed. "It was like being a kid again, running from my brother. But in those days the attic was full of stuff. Today, all I had to duck behind was a chimney."

"You … you used to live here?" Lily asked.

"Oh yeah." The woman stood up and looked around the dim space as if she could see things Lily couldn't. "And I'm coming to live here again," she added. Then her eyes returned to Lily, studying her. "You're the girl I sang with yesterday, aren't you?"

Was this the woman in the big hat? The woman silhouetted against the sun who had known the rest of the lyrics? Yes. Lily could see it now.

"Wait a minute," Alex stammered. "You o-own this place?"

The woman glanced at Alex. "I do," she said with a shrug.

"Then you must be Melva Winston!" Lily blurted. It all made perfect sense. The woman was the right age. And she looked like somebody who once could have blasted out of town on a motorcycle. "The heir to the Winston estate!"

The woman smiled indulgently at Lily. "Not Melva. Annie."

"Annie?" Lily echoed. "Annie Winston?"

"Melva Anastasia Persephone Winston. But you can call me 'Annie.'"

The girls nodded.

"So you three girls are looking for a place to store some stuff and have your club meetings?" Annie asked. "Is that what I heard from behind my chimney?"

"Actually, there are six of us," Lily explained. "But we do need a place to store our stuff. We've been collecting it for a long time. This would be such a great place."

Alex and Kate nodded.

"Hmm," the woman said, reaching to catch a white animal that sprang suddenly and silently out of the shadows.

The girls leapt back.

"You startled them, Rabbit," Annie said. She rubbed the top of the creature's head with her chin, and turned around, rocking it as if the white thing were a baby. "You're a bad, bad boy," she crooned. "A bad boy."

The creature began to growl. A low, rumbling growl.

"Is that a rabbit that growls?" Alex said, her voice going higher.

"Oh, no. No, no, no." Annie rocked and hummed, bringing the bundle in her arms over for the girls to see. "The White Rabbit is a cat."

Lily had never seen such a white cat. Skin showed through at the edges of the cat's ears, making them seem pink.

"He has one blue eye and one green eye," Annie said.

The girls drew close to peer at the cat's eyes in the dim light. He stretched out his neck to smell Kate's fingers. Kate rubbed the side of the kitty's mouth where his whiskers grew. The cat growled more deeply. The girls giggled.

"He likes you," Annie pronounced. "He only growls when somebody he likes rubs his whiskers."

"Why do you call him 'Rabbit'?" Lily asked. "That's a funny name for a cat."

Annie looked at Lily as she opened her arms and let the creature spring out of them. "Well," she began, brushing the front of her shirt, "he's named for a shop I used to own called The White Rabbit."

Lily remembered the tattoo Elizabeth had seen on Annie's shoulder.

"What kind of shop?" Alex asked.

Annie didn't answer. She asked her own question. "Would you girls like to look after Rabbit for a few days? I need to make a trip. He could stay up here, if you'd just feed him, bring fresh water a couple of times each day and spend a little time with him."

Lily looked at her friends. What would their parents say if they knew the girls were visiting an empty, abandoned house twice a day?

"You won't be alone," Annie added quickly. "I've arranged for a lady from town. Catherine O'Leary will come every day to clean and wash windows and start setting things right. She'll be here in the morning. But she's hideously allergic to cats. So Rabbit will have to stay in the attic. My attorney may also be here from time to time."

Lily knew Ms. O'Leary. She went to their church. "Do you think we could have our Silly Stuff Club meetings up here?" Lily asked. "Maybe move in a little of our stuff?"

"Sure," Annie said. "It's time this old crypt had some

girls in it again. And whatever stuff you've collected won't be a grain of sand in this old desert of a house."

Great! That solved the whole Silly Stuff Club problem. They had the owner's permission. They could move their stuff in gradually over the summer. They would have total privacy, and a really cool cat. He could be their club cat. A kind of mascot.

Annie was so nice! So beautiful, in a way. Tiny tattoo and all.

Chapter 8

That night, the Silly Stuff Club e-mailed furiously. They would take care of The White Rabbit in shifts—Lily, Sarah, and AnaMaria on the first morning shift. And with each trip, the girls would haul some silly stuff from the carriage house. Discreetly, of course, as Elizabeth reminded them.

The next morning, in the rain, Lily and Sarah wrestled one end of the wire dressmaker's dummy through the sodden weeds toward the gardener's entrance.

"I hope it doesn't rust," Sarah fretted, breathing hard. "It's a good thing my mom had a dentist appointment and didn't see us. She would have wondered why we were taking a dressmaker's dummy out in the rain."

Lily hoped it didn't rust, too. The rain had been only a mist when they left the Carsons' carriage house. Now it was falling hard enough to sting, and her shoes made annoying *smack!* and *slurp!* sounds as she walked. Sarah, whose legs were much shorter than Lily's and who was heavier, panted as they lugged the dummy.

AnaMaria carried old issues of *National Geographic* with really neat pictures of people from other lands in them. She had tucked the magazines under her shirt, but her shirt was turning dark with the rain. "I'm going to run," she said. "I'll see you on the back porch."

It was hard to run with a dressmaker's dummy, so Lily and Sarah plodded on, listening to the thunder roll. Ahead, AnaMaria vanished through the gardener's gate.

When Lily and Sarah finally got to the back porch, AnaMaria was talking to a pretty, middle-aged woman. Lily recognized her as Ms. O'Leary from their church.

"Girls," Ms. O'Leary said, opening her arms in a welcoming gesture. "Annie said you'd be here to see after the cat. You're wet!"

No kidding. Lily laid down her end of the dressmaker's dummy and nodded for Sarah to do the same.

"The poor thing must have starved," Ms. O'Leary said, looking at the dummy. "Look, she doesn't have a bit of skin on her bones."

Sarah giggled, her sandy red hair waving tightly in the rain, her brown eyes smiling. "She's hungry," she said.

"Well, bring her in," Ms. O'Leary said. "I'm cleaning the kitchen, so there's no food to be cooked. But I knew you were coming, so I brought a bit of cake leftover from my little granddaughter's birthday party."

Lily and Sarah hauled the dummy through the mudroom

and into the kitchen. Ms. O'Leary had an army of spray-on, shake-on, pour-on, and rub-on cleaning products spread out on the counter.

Lily sneezed at the chemical smells.

"Sorry," Ms. O'Leary said, pointing to an old stove. "That's the bad smell, right there. That oven hasn't been cleaned since Hansel and Gretel."

Lily sneezed again.

"Here," Ms. O'Leary said, handing them a cardboard plate. "Take the cake and run on up to the attic. The kitty is probably wondering where you are."

When they opened the attic door, The White Rabbit marched up with the authority of a guard cat and sniffed their wet socks.

"Meet The White Rabbit," Lily said to her friends.

After they'd passed inspection, the cat led them to the small mound of cat food, bowls, water bottles, and kitty litter that Annie had left near one of the dormers.

In the dimness, Lily could barely read the note.

In the a.m., ⅛ cup of canned and ⅛ cup of dried; in the p.m., ⅛ cup of dried. Fresh water every day. Don't forget the litter box. Back before long.

Thanks! Annie.

PS. Ask Ms. O'Leary if you need anything.

While AnaMaria measured and stirred cat food, Lily said, "Wanna bet I can make this cat growl?"

"Cats don't growl," Sarah said.

48

Lily scooped up The White Rabbit and stroked one of the little mounds on either side of his mouth.

The deep, rowdy rumble made AnaMaria drop the spoon. She stared at the cat, then at Lily. "You're making that noise, right?" she accused.

Lily stroked The White Rabbit's magic spot and held him close to AnaMaria. "Now listen," she said. She stopped stroking and Rabbit settled into a demure purr.

Sarah giggled. "I never. It's like pushing an on and off button."

While The White Rabbit ate, AnaMaria found a string hanging down from a shaded overhead bulb. When she pulled it, a cone of light lit the girls.

"What a fabulous place for a clubhouse!" AnaMaria breathed.

"And so private," Sarah said. "We could talk about anything up here. Oh, I wish I wasn't moving away! I'll miss you guys so much!"

"Then there's only one thing we can do," AnaMaria said. "And that's turn it into the most beautiful, magical, wonderful clubhouse before you move to Chattanooga."

"So where do we begin?" Lily asked. AnaMaria's way of making things beautiful seemed as magical as The White Rabbit's growl.

"Right here," AnaMaria said. "Under the light. First we need a rug. Did you see the beautiful art deco rug at the bottom of the stairs?"

"'Art deco'?" Sarah repeated. "What's 'art deco'?"

"It was a beautiful style of decorating back in the 1920s

and '30s. Just about the time the Winstons were getting really rich. Furniture had very simple shapes then. And they used lots of triangles and circles. This house is full of art deco treasures."

"Treasures?" Sarah repeated again.

"The Winstons had a ton of money, so I'll bet some of the stuff is very valuable."

"Maybe that's why crazy old Dr. Winston put barbed wire on the wall," Lily said.

AnaMaria shrugged. "Maybe. But let's ask Ms. O'Leary if we can vacuum the rug and bring it up."

They found Ms. O'Leary in the kitchen and brought her to look at the rug.

Ms. O'Leary nodded. "Annie wants you to make yourselves comfortable. She said it was good to see grandchildren of friends she'd grown up with." Ms. O'Leary produced an ancient vacuum that screamed like a dying brontosaurus when the girls turned it on.

Beneath the dust, as AnaMaria had promised, Lily saw a beautiful turquoise and black pattern of circles and triangles come alive.

"Wow," she and Sarah breathed.

"Ms. O'Leary, are there treasures in this house?" Sarah asked as she rolled up the rug for the trip to the attic.

Ms. O'Leary looked at them rather suddenly over the tops of her glasses. "Why do you ask?" she queried after a moment.

AnaMaria touched one of the tables in the hallway. Even under the grime, it glowed with a beautiful inlay that Lily

50

thought looked like ivory.

"Some of these things are so fine," AnaMaria said, her eyes bright with appreciation. "Surely they're treasures."

"Oh yes! I see what you mean now. Furniture and things. Well yes, I suppose they are treasures. Of course, one person's treasures are another person's trash, I always say. Now, my daughter loves to go to garage sales and flea markets. …"

And Ms. O'Leary rattled on about slightly used clothing that only cost a dollar or two until Lily wondered if she had intentionally changed the subject.

After they unrolled the rug under the light and dreamed for a while about how the place would look when it was done, they went downstairs again.

"We'll be back this evening to feed The White Rabbit," Lily told Ms. O'Leary.

As they walked past Eli's, the outdoor umbrellas dripped. But Lily was pretty sure she saw Kate's Texas-talkin' visitor through the window.

Chapter 9

That night, as Lily was brushing her teeth, her mother called up the stairs, "Phone for you, Honey. But it's 10:30, so be quick."

Lily ran across the hall and picked up the phone in her bedroom.

"Hello?" She heard the click as her mother hung up.

"L-Lily?" Sarah's voice was shaking.

"Sarah? What's wrong?"

Sarah whispered, "You know how I sometimes go out my window onto the roof just to get away from my bratty brothers? Well, Lily! There is a light jumping around at the old Winston place! I can see it shining up over the wall!"

"It's probably just Ms. O'Leary staying late to do some cleaning," Lily said. She drew a stroke of Purple Paradise nail enamel down the center of one fingernail. Her sister would be really annoyed if she knew Lily was using her stuff.

"Huh-uh. I saw Ms. O'Leary leave a couple of hours ago," Sarah murmured. "I was out in the yard and she waved at me as she passed. Plus, this light isn't like that. This light moves."

"Lightning bugs?" Lily said.

"Not hardly!" Sarah's annoyance showed in her voice. "OK, if you don't take me seriously, I'll stop telling you. But I'm worried about The White Rabbit, and I'm going to go make sure he's OK."

Lily couldn't let Sarah go by herself—not with Sarah's wild, poetic imagination.

"Not without me, you're not," Lily said. "Just wait until I get there. I'll meet you at the end of your drive, OK?"

"OK," Sarah said. "But hurry. Ride your bike."

Lily ripped off her pajamas and pulled on a pair of shorts and a T-shirt. Her mother would never let her go out at ten thirty—not even during summer vacation.

"'Night, Mom," she called down the stairs.

"'Night, Honey." Her mother's voice rose over the sound track of a sitcom.

Lily shut her bedroom door and opened her window. In a few seconds, she was onto the porch roof, down the clematis trellis, and across the yard.

She grabbed her bike from the garage and pedaled off. She would meet Sarah, convince her that the light was just a reflection or something, and peek in on The White Rabbit. She'd be back in bed before her mom's TV program was even over.

Chapter 10

The rain had stopped. A cool, fresh breeze blew Lily's hair away from her face as she pedaled through town on Market. Some teenagers, their car doors open, hung out around the square. A Summary police car was parked in the deserted parking lot of the Kroger store.

The still-dripping trees sprinkled Lily's shoulders as she pedaled up Summary Lane. The breeze drove away the last of the clouds and a round moon peered at her.

Sarah waited, hunkered down by the mailbox. Lily thought Sarah was a clump of tall grass until she stood up.

"I thought you'd never get here," Sarah said, keeping her voice low. She picked her bike up from the ditch and the girls pedaled off together. Their tires hissed on the wet pavement.

"It's dark out here," Lily said. "No streetlights."

"Not dark enough," Sarah insisted, her voice tense. "Look. Can't you see the light flickering behind the wall?"

Lily squinted. Not really.

Well … maybe she did see something. Just a pale movement—patches of light bouncing off the trees now and then.

"It's the moonlight reflecting off the fish pond."

Sarah snorted. "That fish pond has two inches of algae on it. Plus, the moon wasn't out when I saw the light the first time."

Something charged through the tall grass at the side of the road. The shrieks and yowls that followed made the hair on Lily's arms stand up.

"Cats," Sarah whispered. "Oh dear. What if something happens to The White Rabbit? What if we're too late?"

Too late for what? Lily wished she'd had her mom drive them out. Absolutely nobody in the whole entire world knew where she and Sarah were going. But they were almost there now. They'd just run in, check on Rabbit, hop on their bikes, and ride home.

As they leaned their bikes against the wall outside the gardener's gate, an owl hooted gently, questioningly from a tree in the field.

"Hello, owl," Lily called softly, trying to make friends with the night.

Not until she was leading the way among the ghostly garden statuary did she realize that the gardener's gate hadn't squeaked when they opened and closed it. It had always squeaked before. It had squeaked that very morning.

Hideously.

For the first time, Lily felt a shimmer of true fear. What if somebody really was inside the grounds? As if a thousand tiny fingers moved up Lily's body from her feet to her head, she felt the hair on her body rise.

She stopped. Sarah bumped into her and let out a little shriek. "The light! See, I told you!"

It danced briefly and palely out one of the windows and bounced off the canopy of huge old trees that overhung the house.

"I see it," Lily admitted.

Maybe Ms. O'Leary had left a night light on. Maybe a raccoon was in the house and somehow moving the light, making it swing and move. Maybe …

Holding hands, she and Sarah crept up the porch steps. Before she even looked for the spare key in the storage box, Lily tried the door. It was unlocked. Had Ms. O'Leary forgotten to lock up when she left?

"I don't see anybody," Sarah whispered. "And I don't hear anybody either. Should we turn on a light?"

"If we turn on a light, other people might see, then we'd be in so-o-o-o much trouble. My mom thinks I'm sleeping in my bed."

"Yeah," Sarah said. "I get your point."

The girls crept through the kitchen, the butler's pantry, the dining room, and into the foyer. The moonlight through the windows cast deep shadows. The tall trees, their leaves wobbling in the wind, stirred the shadows until Lily felt almost dizzy in the darkness.

"Let's just check on The White Rabbit and leave," she said. "If anybody was here, they don't seem to be here now."

They went up the grand stairway, then down the narrow hall and up the flights of stairs to the attic. The White Rabbit was curled on his pillow in the moonlight. He raised his head to look at them, made a half-purr of greeting, shifted positions, and relaxed, shutting his eyes once more.

"See?" Lily said. "He's fine."

"Well, thank goodness," Sarah said.

"Yeah. We can go home now."

The moon went behind a cloud and the house dimmed until the girls could barely see the pale shapes of the windows.

"Wish we had a flashlight," Lily said.

In the kitchen, they made their way toward the door, touching the counters and groping in the darkness.

"Just about there," Lily whispered. She longed to run, but she was afraid she'd crash into something, or lose Sarah in the darkness.

Then, with an intake of breath that was almost a scream, Sarah grabbed Lily. A shape darker than darkness rose up tall—taller than any human being.

Lily screamed. Sarah screamed.

The thing had two points on its top, like a vampire.

"Run!" Lily cried, clutching Sarah's hand.

Silently the great, tall, dark thing collapsed and disappeared.

"Run, run, run!" Lily cried again. They were almost to the door.

Then they were through the door, fleeing through the garden, leaping over fallen statues.

"Look out for the fish pond!" Sarah gasped.

Across the grounds they flew, through the gardener's gate that didn't squeak anymore, racing along the wall. They didn't stop until they stumbled over their bikes.

Back on the road, Lily pedaled so fast her feet nearly flew off. She could hear Sarah gasping for breath behind her.

When they were almost at Sarah's house, a vehicle growled out of the darkness behind them, gathering speed, bearing down on them. The girls were caught in the headlights. As the vehicle shot past, Lily saw only that it was a dark truck. And it had to have come from the old Winston estate, because that's where the road ended.

Chapter 11

Lily called an emergency club meeting the next morning. Everybody gathered in the old clubhouse, which seemed to Lily to be a tiny bit emptier since they'd carried a few things up to Annie's attic already.

But after their experience last night, Lily didn't know if she ever wanted to go back in that house again.

"It was awful," Sarah breathed, after Lily had finished telling the rest of the club what had happened to them.

"Unbelievably awful," Lily added, remembering the huge figure that had loomed, then shrunk, seeming to vanish into the shadows. "Something almost got us!"

"Well, should we call the police?" AnaMaria asked.

"It was dark, right?" Kate asked Lily.

"Yeah, except for a little moonlight."

"So would the police think you're just a couple of silly

girls seeing Dracula out of season?" Kate looked around the room. "Maybe we ought to find out a little more first. Go back to the house in the daylight and look around."

"Find some clues," Elizabeth agreed. "Some real evidence that an intruder was there."

So Lily and her friends once more trekked out to the old Winston place, this time in the sunshine. When they got there, the gates were wide open. Hacked-back grapevine and weeds made a mound beside the drive. A man who had helped put new gutters on Lily's family's house last summer was repairing hinges.

"Fine morning," he said. "Fresh after the rain."

"And we needed the rain," AnaMaria said politely.

As they walked through the gates, Elizabeth said, "Cool. We can go in the front now and skip the itchy weeds." She was wearing new black platform shoes which she described simply as "fabulously pricey."

Inside, Ms. O'Leary, wearing yellow rubber gloves, was on her knees, scouring the tile in the front hallway.

As Lily and Sarah recounted their adventure to her, Lily began to fear that they were making a mistake. Wouldn't a grown-up insist they should call the police?

But, to Lily's surprise, after Ms. O'Leary had heard them out, she simply looked sympathetic and asked the girls if they'd like to search the house.

"Great idea," Lily said. "See, this all happened by the basement door. So maybe we could look down there."

"There might be clues," Elizabeth said, her eyes sparkling with the mystery.

"Yes," Ms. O'Leary said. "There might be." She pulled off her rubber gloves. "Just let me get a lantern, girls. The basement doesn't have electricity, you know. Annie has asked me to call about having an electrician come. Dark as a tar pit down there. Damp as a dungeon, too."

Lily shivered, but Alex nudged her. "Six girls together are invincible," she whispered.

A few minutes later, Ms. O'Leary led the way, holding a lantern high as they inched down a twisting flight of narrow, wobbly stairs. The smell that rose from the darkness made Lily think of rotten potatoes and dead mice.

Lily's nerves let themselves out in the line of a song she'd sung at camp. "One dark night, when we were all in bed, Old Mother Leary left a lantern in the shed. . . ."

When nobody joined in with her, she ended with a self-conscious giggle. "Be careful with that lantern, Ms. O'Leary," she said.

Maybe it was her imagination, but she thought the woman shot her a dirty look.

"Girls, I'll leave the lantern with you here," she said, thrusting the light into Lily's hands. "I'll get back to my cleaning." And she turned toward the open doorway into the kitchen.

"I think you offended her," Sarah whispered as Ms. O'Leary disappeared through the rectangle of light at the top of the stairs. Then that light disappeared too, and the girls were in total darkness except for the weak glow cast by the lantern.

"I know." Lily was sorry. She had just been making nervous chatter.

"So what's the rest of the song?" Elizabeth asked as they trailed down the next flight of stairs behind Lily.

Lily sang the first line again and finished the song. "And when the cow kicked it over, she winked her eye and said, 'There'll be a hot time in the old town tonight!'"

"Fire, fire, fire!" Alex joined in with her on the last line. "I remember that song now. It's about the great Chicago fire."

Lily stepped off the bottom step onto dirt, nearly losing her balance. The lantern swung wildly as she grabbed for Sarah's hand.

"Stop," Elizabeth commanded. "Look for footprints before we make our own."

Lily held the lantern high and moved it as far as she could without making footprints.

"Nothing," Kate said. "So if your spook came down here, either he floats on the air or he stayed on the steps and came back up when you were gone."

Lily swallowed, the terror of last night returning. "Let's get out of here," she said in a low voice. "There's nothing here but mold." She shivered. Who knew what could be buried in the dirt?

Upstairs, Ms. O'Leary seemed to have her good humor back and to have forgiven Lily for blaming the great Chicago fire on somebody who might have been an ancestor.

"You girls asked about treasure yesterday," she said, smiling as if she had candy in her pockets. "Have you ever heard the rumors about the old doctor going mad and hiding things around the place? Some say he hid a fortune in cash. Others say he didn't hide anything more valuable than some ratty old papers. And others say it's a bunch of hooey—that folks in Summary don't have enough to talk about." Ms. O'Leary gazed around the vastness of the entryway, the tall ceilings, the nooks and crannies. "But it makes you wonder, doesn't it?"

The girls looked at each other.

"We'd better go see about The White Rabbit," Lily finally said.

Up in Annie's attic, they toured the place, looking carefully behind all the chimneys to make sure they were really and truly alone.

"Look!" Lily exclaimed, tugging Sarah over to one of the dormers. "Look at that pickup down there."

And as she and Sarah watched, a shiny, dark blue truck turned around at the end of Summary Lane. A man inside, who Lily thought looked familiar, seemed to be leaning out the window and talking to somebody on his cell phone.

"Kate," Lily called. "Come here. Isn't that your Texas-talkin' man?"

"Yep," Kate said. "Wonder what he's doing out here, driving all slow and looking around?"

"The truck that almost ran us over last night was dark," Lily told them.

"Yeah, but we were in the dark, too," Sarah reminded her. "It could have been anybody."

"I suppose so," Lily said.

Giving up their search, satisfied that they were safe and alone in Annie's attic, the girls finally settled onto the beautiful art deco rug in the cozy cone of light from the overhead bulb.

Sarah took The White Rabbit onto her lap and began to stroke him.

"So what do you think?" Lily asked. "Do you think the lights last night could have been somebody looking for whatever old Doc Winston might have hidden?"

"That would mean we interrupted a burglary," Sarah breathed, her hand pausing in mid-stroke.

The White Rabbit purred.

When the girls looked at him, he closed his eyes, seeming to ponder the thought.

"Well, if there's treasure hidden in this house," AnaMaria said, "why shouldn't we find it? We can give it to Annie to thank her for letting us use the attic."

"And think how famous we'd be," Alex said. "Heroes!"

"We could just casually look around a little," Elizabeth said, "as we come each day to take care of Rabbit and move our stuff in."

The White Rabbit opened his eyes and purred again. Then he quit abruptly, his eyes fixed on the door.

When the girls turned to look, they saw nothing, but Lily thought she smelled Lysol as they left the attic.

When they got downstairs, Ms. O'Leary was nowhere to be seen, but someone was standing outside the open front door on the porch.

Lily recognized him immediately by his height and odd, narrow, fishy face. It was the lawyer, Mr. Tuppin, the one Elizabeth said was called "Snapper."

"Hullo," Lily said, going to the door. The rest of her posse followed her.

"Hullo," Mr. Tuppin said, frowning. "I didn't realize that Ms. Winston had … children … living here."

Lily drew herself up to her full height, which was nowhere near his, but still … "We're Annie's friends," she said.

"A bit young, aren't you?" he asked, his mouth making an extra-fishy O shape.

"We're looking after her cat," AnaMaria said, stepping forward to stand by Lily. "And you would be?"

"I'm her attorney. I've come to drop off some papers that Ms. Winston asked for."

"You can leave them with us," Lily said, opening the screen door and holding out her hand. "We'll make sure she gets them."

He frowned, his brows meeting in the middle of his narrow face. "Very well," he finally said. "I suppose so." And he handed Lily a single sealed manila envelope.

"We'll give it to her," Lily said.

He zipped his briefcase, bent his lips as if to smile, nodded once, wheeled, and walked off the porch. As he went through the gate, Lily heard the handyman say, "Nice buggy, Art."

The lawyer raised his hand in acknowledgement, then slid into the red BMW convertible.

Chapter 12

"Who can do lunch at Eli's?" Elizabeth asked as they walked through the gates.

"My mom's taking the afternoon off and we're going to paint the rooms over the garage for my grandmother," AnaMaria said. "You should see the colors I picked! No wall will be the same. It will be so bright and festive for her when she gets here from Mexico."

"I have an orthodontist's appointment," Sarah said. "Did I tell you I might be getting braces before the summer is over?"

"I've got a softball game," Alex said. "Sorry."

"Sure," Kate said. "I can go to lunch."

Lily had planned to work on a new craft project that she'd ordered, but lunch at Eli's sounded like even more fun.

"There's your Texas-talkin' man," she murmured to Kate

a few minutes later as they went inside Eli's to get their food. He was sitting in the corner booth by himself.

"Let's just call him 'Tex,'" Kate whispered, "for ease of reference."

She smiled and nodded at Tex, who nodded back after a second.

After they'd settled around a table on the patio, Elizabeth slipped a silver ring off her finger. "My parents sent me this from Egypt," she said, twisting it so that it glinted in the sunshine.

The ring was lovely. The strands of silver twisted together reminded Lily of a complicated knot.

"Watch!" Elizabeth commanded. She dropped the ring onto the table. It separated into several pieces of curved silver linked together.

"It's a puzzle!" Kate said, picking it up. "I love puzzles."

"I know. Would you like to borrow it?"

"Sure!" Kate started twisting the circles of silver together.

"Hello, Elizabeth."

It was the guy they'd seen the first day with Annie. Les Dudley, the handyman.

"How are your parents?" he asked. "Does your mom like the shelves in her closet?"

"I think so," Elizabeth said. "Though she's hardly ever home to use them."

What would life be like, staying most of the time with a housekeeper while your parents gallivanted around the globe?

"I'm going out to the old Winston place this afternoon," he said. "I guess some wiring is needed in the basement?" He looked at the girls questioningly over the tops of his steel-rimmed glasses.

Why was he asking them?

"Catherine O'Leary told me you girls had been down there looking around. It must have been kind of hard to see without a good light."

"Yeah," Lily admitted.

"Dirt floors?" he asked.

Lily nodded.

Les Dudley rocked back on his heels. "I haven't been in one of those old dirt-floored cellars for many years. See anything interesting down there?"

Lily exchanged looks with Kate and Elizabeth.

"Nope," she said.

"Guess I better head on out. See you girls later. Give my best to your folks," he said, nodding to Elizabeth.

When he was out of earshot, Kate raised her eyebrows. "Now what was *that* all about?"

Lily and Elizabeth shrugged.

"Why would Ms. O'Leary even mention us to him?" Kate asked.

Lily and Elizabeth shrugged again.

"Weird," Kate concluded.

Lily and Elizabeth nodded. "Totally," Elizabeth agreed.

"Well, the day is way past half-gone," Elizabeth said when they finally finished their sandwiches and cheesecake and had discussed the merits of Purple Poison nail enamel over Poppy Pink. "And you and I have the duty with The White Rabbit later," she said, looking at Lily. "Do you want to haul some silly stuff, then just hang out for a while until it's time to feed The White Rabbit?"

"I need to practice my French," Kate said. "Dad and I have class tonight. I so wish that he and our French teacher would get together. They'd make such a cute couple."

"Later, then," Lily said as she and Elizabeth went one way and Kate the other.

"What shall we take?" Lily asked, unlocking the door to the old carriage house.

Elizabeth hung a hula hoop around her neck. "Hardly makes a fashion statement, does it?" she asked, pirouetting. "But I'll carry this and this." She picked up an old tin coffee can that had most of the paint rubbed off, though the girls could still make out "Butternut, the coffee delicious" on the lid.

"Right," Lily said, "and I'll carry these." She gathered up an armload of books with quaint-looking children in them that Alex had found in her grandmother's old chicken house.

Chapter 13

"Do you think Annie would mind if we borrowed a bookcase or something?" Lily asked Ms. O'Leary, whom they found polishing ornate molding in the huge dining room.

"There must be a million pieces of furniture in this house," Ms. O'Leary decided. "If you can carry it, I doubt Annie would mind you taking it up to the attic."

"Come on then," Lily said to Elizabeth. "Let's look for something."

"This is just like shopping," Elizabeth giggled, drifting into a room that must once have been a parlor or the front drawing room.

Ornate baseboard, twelve inches high, ran around the edges of the octagonal room. Carved molding lined the tops of the walls and extended down from the corners.

Elizabeth breathed a sigh of appreciation. "This is like shopping in a big old museum—maybe the Metropolitan Museum of Art in New York City. Ever been there?" she asked Lily.

Lily shook her head as she surveyed the room. "I've been all over Summary, Indiana, though."

Elizabeth rolled her eyes. "In summary, you are not well traveled."

Lily groaned. "That's terrible."

"I know," Elizabeth said. Then she pointed to an enormous piece of furniture with shelves behind beveled glass doors. "That would be perfect for the attic if it wasn't ten feet tall and didn't weigh as much as an SUV."

"Imagine trying to carry that up to the attic," Lily sighed. "But look, Liz." She pointed to an oddity in the molding that ran down the corner beside the glass-fronted cabinet. "It's a crack."

Just as Lily couldn't resist pulling thread on a loose button, she couldn't resist putting her fingers in the crack and tugging. Just to see what would happen.

Elizabeth pressed her fingers over her mouth as the molding pivoted silently outward into the living room, revealing another door.

Lily shook her head. She had to be seeing things.

"Wild," Elizabeth breathed. "We've found a secret door."

They heard the rhythmic scrubbing of Ms. O'Leary's brush on the foyer floor, and the occasional banging of the handyman still working on the enormous front gates.

"What do you suppose is on the other side?" Elizabeth whispered.

And was it locked? That was the question.

Lily tried it. The knob turned and the door swung inward with a creak.

"Shhhhhhhh!" Elizabeth said.

Lily motioned Elizabeth in, and then she swung the molding back in place and closed the door.

The dust made Lily cough. She buried her face in the crook of her arm to muffle the noise. But behind all that wood, they could probably play the *1812 Overture* with real cannons and nobody would hear them.

Faint seams of light showed on the opposite wall. Groping her way across the low-ceilinged room, Lily realized that there were windows shuttered from the outside.

She felt through the dust and spider webs and who-knew-what other gross stuff for the latch. "Help me lift this," she grunted.

With much bumping and squeaking, the window went up. The latch to the heavy board shutters was on the inside. Lily slid the bolt back and pushed the shutter open enough to let in some light.

Then she could see the hooded lamp on the desk, shrouded in cobweb streamers. She made herself reach through the strands and find the chain. She pulled it, and light washed the desktop.

Elizabeth, who was right at her elbow, blew the dust off a heavy old book and opened it. "Just some kind of bookkeeping ledger," she said. "But look at these newspapers,

Lily. Look at the funny skirts the women have on."

"Look at the date," Lily pointed out. "Wednesday, June 17—"

"Hey, that's today!" Elizabeth exclaimed.

"—1925," Lily finished. And she shivered, looking at Elizabeth.

Elizabeth shrugged. "Coincidences happen?" she said, her voice rising with the question and her eyes huge.

They paged through the newspaper, *The Summary Ledger*. Somebody named Scopes arrested in Tennessee for teaching evolution. Something called "radiovision." More people in really strange-looking clothes.

"Look," Lily said, "here's something about Dr. Winston in a paper from 1935."

Together they read the front-page story about how the good and talented doctor had recently sold some patents for a great deal of money. The article was circled in ink that had long since turned brown. Lily could barely make out the scribbled words, "And wisely invested ... The fools!"

"We're in his office," Elizabeth breathed. She looked around at the clutter, the stacks of books and papers. "But why is it so secret?"

"Because he was a little nuts," Lily replied. She gazed around the dim, dust-encrusted space. If the office were cleaned up it would probably look exactly as the old doctor had left it. "Remember what Ms. O'Leary said."

"That he hid his money? You think he hid it here?" Elizabeth asked. Then, after a second, she mused, "I wonder if Annie knows about this place."

"Look at it," Lily said, with a gesture. "*Nobody* knows about this place."

"Except us," Elizabeth said.

Lily nodded.

"It would be cool to find the money for Annie," Elizabeth said. "Plus we'd be a little famous. They'd write about us and put it in the paper. I think we should look around."

They opened drawers and doors and stuck their hands into the darkness of pigeonholes where living creatures might lurk, but Lily tried not to think about it. Despite their efforts, they found only veterinary journals and volumes of research notes that meant absolutely nothing to them.

"Look at this, Liz," Lily said, pointing to a deep wooden filing drawer labeled simply "The Farm."

There were photos in the drawer of a sprawling farm with a house and outbuildings. It all looked a little familiar to Lily, as if she'd gone by such a place—though she couldn't think where.

There were pictures of horses, with curious notations beneath them. Dates. Words the girls didn't understand.

"Maybe it's Latin," Elizabeth said.

"I wonder if the farm is around here?" Lily asked. "I wonder if it's still in the Winston family?"

Elizabeth shrugged. "We could ask Ms. O."

The girls carefully closed the shutter and the window, turned off the lamp, and eased open the panel a slit. The room was empty.

"It's safe," Lily whispered, pushing back the panel the rest of the way and stepping out into the room. "Listen.

Who's Ms. O'Leary talking to?"

The sound of two voices discussing outlets, fuse boxes, and voltages drifted back to them from the front door.

"Les Dudley," Elizabeth said.

And then the voices dropped to a quiet murmur, almost a whisper, which Lily couldn't make out.

Shortly, Ms. O'Leary began conversing in a normal tone.

"OK, just let me get my toolbox," Les Dudley answered, "and I'll go down and have a look."

Lily and Elizabeth showed themselves into the foyer. Lily didn't know why she felt guilty. She hadn't been the one whispering.

"Well, have you girls found any furniture for your cozy place in the attic?" Ms. O'Leary asked.

"We're still looking," Lily said. And then she decided that if she was going to be guilty of trying to eavesdrop, she might as well be guilty of a little white lie, too. "Ms. O'Leary," she asked, making her eyes wide with innocence, "my grandfather said that the Winstons used to own a beautiful horse farm somewhere around here. Do they still? I love horses!"

Ms. O'Leary pulled her yellow rubber gloves back on. "They still own it. It's just a couple of miles out on the Old Wabash Road. But there aren't any horses there anymore. They were all sold off after the old vet died. And some of them were in sad and sorry shape is what I heard."

Chapter 14

Sad and sorry shape. Lily tossed and turned, her window up, listening to the tree frogs. The bells from St. James Episcopal Church bonged twelve times. Midnight already.

Had old Dr. Winston been so crazy in his latter years that he'd done inhumane experiments on horses? Grafted goats' heads onto horses' bodies? Produced five-legged colts that barked?

She sat up and fluffed her pillow, trying to drive away the midnight thoughts. Silly, spooky thoughts. She'd been hanging around the old Winston place too long. That was the problem. Poking around in dark cellars and dusty secret rooms, listening to tall tales from Ms. O'Leary. What she needed was some fresh air, a change of scenery, a nice bike ride into the country.

And so she pedaled out to the Old Wabash Road

the next morning, AnaMaria and Alex beside her. They bubbled with questions about the hidden office that she and Elizabeth had discovered the day before.

"If he really was nuts," Alex said, "maybe the rumors are right. Maybe he did hide all his money."

"But wouldn't even a crazy person want to look after his family?" AnaMaria asked. "Wouldn't he want his kids and grandkids to be able to find the money someday?"

"And maybe they did," Alex said. "Maybe it's all been found already."

There was almost no traffic on the Old Wabash Road, so the girls were able to ride side by side. Fresh air, exercise, and good friends. Just what Lily needed.

"Annie is his granddaughter," Lily reasoned, "his only heir. And she doesn't seem like somebody who has found a lot of money."

"Well, in that case," Alex said, pulling in behind Lily so a pickup could pass them, "maybe he left a clue for us."

That was what Lily was secretly hoping for.

When they came around a curve and saw the farm, she recognized the place immediately from the pictures she and Elizabeth had examined yesterday. But the property had a neglected look now. The white board fences had fallen over in places. The smaller outbuildings were hidden behind tall wildflowers and overgrown with vines. And the barn sagged like a sway-backed mule, the roof dipping dangerously. Strands of frayed rope dangled from the tall branch of an oak tree. Maybe it had once been Annie's swing.

Farther back down the lane, a house, the white paint

peeling, sat between two twisted cottonwoods in a carelessly mowed yard.

The girls dropped their bikes beside the road and walked up the short lane to the barn. In the quiet of the deep country, Lily could hear AnaMaria and Alex breathing beside her. Maybe she could even hear the old barn sagging—a whispery creak of wood and nails.

Caaaaaa! A huge crow scolded them from where it was pecking something near the open entrance of the barn, and then flew, beating its wings.

AnaMaria stood with her hand over her heart. "Scared me!" she exclaimed.

Inside the barn, dust motes floated in the sun that pierced the bare ribs of the roof joists.

Suddenly Alex screamed, making Lily jump so high she bit her tongue. And AnaMaria fled out the door.

Lily looked where a paralyzed Alex was pointing. "Aratararatarat," she chattered. "A nasty rat!"

A small gray mouse sat in the dust, staring at them.

Lily couldn't believe it. Brave, bold Alex was scared of mice!

"Shoo," she instructed, clapping her hands, and the mouse vanished into the shadows.

Alex, still pale, backed out the door, her gaze swinging from side to side to make sure she wasn't going to be ambushed by an army of mice.

Lily didn't let herself laugh. Everybody was scared of something.

"I am not going back in that barn," Alex vowed as she

backed fifty feet out the door.

"How about the house?" Lily proposed.

Alex shook her head. "You can go in if you want to. I'm going to stand right here and make sure I don't see any more mice."

"Well, since we rode all the way out here, let's take a quick look around." Lily looked at AnaMaria, who nodded.

Lily and AnaMaria went up the steps and across the wooden porch. Lily knocked.

"I don't think anybody lives here," AnaMaria said after a while. "Look at the flyspecks on the windows. And look how something has made a nest in the corner." She pointed to her feet.

So Lily tried the door. Locked.

"You don't suppose the key Annie gave us to the other house might fit this door too, do you?" AnaMaria said.

Lily got the key out of her pocket and tried it.

"You're brilliant," she told AnaMaria as they let themselves in.

AnaMaria shrugged modestly.

Inside, the house seemed to push down on them with musty heat and a faint whiff of something else. What was it? Something fresher. Something that wafted away before Lily could identify it.

She wiped sweat off her face.

Dust powdered all the surfaces, seeming to muffle sound. As the girls walked from room to room, Lily heard only the creak of the old floors beneath their weight and the droning of fat black flies as they banged against the windows.

"It's just an old farmhouse," Lily said after they'd wandered through a few of the rooms. "Hardly anything left in it."

Somebody had moved out most of the furniture long ago. They'd left only a few pieces amidst rolled-up carpets, cardboard boxes of trash, and mouse droppings.

"That's a nice old writing desk," AnaMaria said, pointing to a massive, dark piece of furniture in one corner of a back room. "See, its front drops down to make the desk." She turned a brass key and let down a large wooden flap. Inside were cubbyholes on the right and a separate locked compartment on the left. The key from the front also fit the locked compartment, and Lily watched her open it to reveal bookshelves.

A matched set of leather-bound books bore *Annals of Veterinary Medicine* on their spines.

"A book is missing," Lily said. "Look!"

There was a dust-free footprint of the last book. "It would be W through Z," AnaMaria said. "The other volumes are all here. W for Winston. You suppose the old doctor had an article printed in these *Annals* and somebody swiped it?"

"As dusty as this place is, it couldn't have been too long ago."

"I wonder who took it—and why?" AnaMaria said. "Do you suppose it was a clue?"

Lily shrugged. She slid the other books off the shelves, fanning through them for markings or notes, shaking them to see if anything fell out.

"We'll probably never know. I have a feeling that somebody beat us to this house," she said. "Probably it's been thoroughly searched already."

"Well, pooh," AnaMaria said. "It would have been so cool to find the money."

"Yeah," Lily agreed. "If it ever even existed."

As they were leaving, AnaMaria spotted some broken crockery in the top of a decaying cardboard box in the living room. "Look," she said. "It's cracked and chipped, but it's kind of pretty."

Lily helped her take out a stack of very old, very dirty china plates. Most of the gilt had worn off the scalloped rims, but the girls could still make out the flowers and farm scenes painted along the edges. Each plate had a different saying lettered in the center.

AnaMaria flipped one of the plates and rubbed off the grime. "It says 'Custom crafted by B Lawton China for Barnaby Winston 1935.'"

1935? Why did that date ring a bell with Lily? And then she had it. "1935 was the year Dr. Winston made his fortune," she told AnaMaria. "Elizabeth and I found a newspaper clipping about it in the secret office."

"So I'll bet he commissioned the plates to celebrate his new fortune." AnaMaria studied the front of the plates. "Where's Kate when we really need her? The lettering is in French."

Lily clumsily stammered through the words on the first plate. "*Je regrette que j'aie seulement une vie pour donner a mon pays.*"

"OK," AnaMaria acknowledged. "Now what does this one say?"

"Well that one says '*C'est une meilleure chose extreme que je fais maintenant que j'ai jamais fait avant,*'" Lily rattled off as if she had the clearest idea what she was saying. "Look, AnaMaria, someone painted over the original saying on this last one."

"Can you read it?" AnaMaria asked.

"I think so. It's something like '*Ha, ha, ha! He, he, he! Parlez-vous francais? Ah oui oui. Cacher dans la vue simple. Regardez le plafond.*'"

"'*Ha, ha, ha? He, he, he?*'" AnaMaria questioned. "That's sort of different. Not like the others."

Lily shrugged. It was all gibberish to her. "But one thing I notice is that the writing on the plate looks the same as the writing on that 1935 newspaper."

"I think we should take these plates and compare the writing," AnaMaria said.

"I agree. They could be a clue. Let's go show Alex."

"What took you so long?" Alex wanted to know, when the girls came to get her. She was still doing her mouse watch. "Did you find anything?"

"Somebody has been here before us, probably," Lily said. "The dust pattern on the shelf of an old writing desk showed a book was recently missing. Hard to tell what else."

"What have you got there?"

"One of these plates we found could be a clue," AnaMaria said, holding it out for Alex to see and explaining the difference on the altered plate.

"Wow!" Alex said.

As the girls were hurrying back down the lane, they saw the man they'd nicknamed Tex. He slowed his pickup and powered down his window, pulling to a stop.

"H'lo, girls. Seems like I see you everywhere."

Odd. He had taken the words right out of Lily's mouth.

"We've not met officially," he said. "Name's Allan Terwho. Out of Texas."

Lily glanced at her friends.

"I don't suppose you happen to know if this old farm is for sale, do you?"

"No," Lily said. "We don't know. Why?"

"Oh, I'm just looking for a place to do some development," Tex said. "Be a good spot. Nothing around but open country. Now the people on the other side of the road"— he pointed to well-kept pastures to the west—"they have a going operation. So naturally they wouldn't want to sell. But it looks like nobody but you girls has been on this farm in the last twenty five years."

He stared at them until Lily clapped at a gnat and said they needed to get going.

The pickup was blocking the end of the lane. The only way the girls could get their bikes out was to go through the ditch, which sprouted a wall of very itchy-looking chigger weed.

But Tex didn't seem to be in a hurry. "See that horse over there?" he mused, pointing to a gray horse walking the neighboring pasture. "Could have stringhalt. Or maybe glanders. People need to take care of their animals." He tapped his fingers on the steering wheel as if he were going to sit there blocking the lane all day.

"Whatcha got there?" he asked, nodding at the plates AnaMaria was carrying.

"Just silly stuff," she said.

For some reason the girls didn't understand, this made him laugh. With a little salute, he powered up his window and drove off, fogging them with dust.

"Stringhalt?" Alex said. "Glanders? What's that?"

"Some kind of veterinary talk, I'll bet," AnaMaria said.

"Do you think he's a vet?" Lily asked. "Or knows something about veterinary medicine? Why would a land developer know about stuff like that?"

"And do you think he said what he did about it looking like nobody had been on this place in twenty five years to cover up for something?" AnaMaria asked.

"Yeah, like maybe he was the one who'd been sneaking around and took the book," Lily said. "And he wanted to throw us off the scent."

"Well, he just made me more sure than ever that something of value really is hidden somewhere," Alex said.

"And we want to find it first," Lily concluded.

Her friends nodded.

Chapter 15

Feeling that time was running out, Lily called another emergency meeting of the Silly Stuff Club—though their race to beat somebody to the treasure didn't feel very silly. Sarah said they couldn't meet in the carriage house that afternoon. A realtor was showing their property and the whole family had to be gone for a couple of hours.

So Lily suggested they meet at the gazebo on the square.

"Look," she explained, when they were all gathered around, "somebody besides us is definitely searching for the money—or whatever the old vet hid." Lily recounted the evidence, holding up a finger. "One. That night Sarah and I went to explore the strange light in the house, somebody was there."

"Somebody acting like Dracula's cousin who wanted to scare us off," Sarah added.

"Two," Lily continued. "This morning when AnaMaria and I explored the old farmhouse, somebody had recently been there and taken W through Z of some veterinary books—which could have had information in it about Dr. Winston. The dust had barely settled."

"Maybe he was still in the house," Sarah gasped.

"Don't say that!" AnaMaria's eyes grew huge at the possibility.

But Lily remembered the peculiar fresh smell that she'd noticed. Had an intruder still been in the house?

"Well, did you find anything?" Kate asked. "See anything that could possibly be a clue?"

Lily watched as AnaMaria proudly produced the three old plates. She had washed them, making the old china gleam. The worn gilt sparkled in the light. "They have French sayings on them," she said, laying them out on a bench. "Maybe you can translate, Kate."

Kate straightened her glasses and leaned her head to one side, thinking.

"Got it!" she finally said, touching the first one.

"What?" a couple of the girls demanded.

"'I regret that I have only one life to give for my country.'"

"I've heard that someplace before," Alex said.

"Sure you have," Kate explained. "We studied it in history. Nathan Hale, the American patriot, said it right before they hung him."

"Yuck!" Alex said.

"And this one," Kate said, pointing to the second plate,

"is almost equally as famous. It's from Dickens's *A Tale of Two Cities*. It translates as 'It is a far better thing that I do now than I have ever done before.' Sidney Carton said that right before they cut off his head."

"Ewwww!" Elizabeth exclaimed.

How Kate could be so smart, Lily didn't know.

But the third plate, with its messy scrawl, seemed to stump even Kate. "This I do not understand," she finally admitted, staring at the plate with the words "*Ha, ha, ha! He, he, he! Parlez-vous francais? A oui oui. Cacher dans la vue simple. Regardez le plafond.*"

"Why? What does it say?" Elizabeth asked. "Isn't it something famous somebody said before they died?"

"I don't think so," Kate said. "It translates roughly something like this. First there's the words indicating laughter—"

"Hey, I got that part right," Elizabeth said. "And don't the next words, '*Parlez vous francaise?*,' mean 'Do you speak French?'"

"And '*A oui oui*' would mean 'Yes, I do,'" Lily decided, realizing that maybe she knew more French than she thought.

"So what does the rest of it mean?" Sarah asked.

"Something like this: 'Hide in plain sight. Look at the ceiling.'"

"'Hide in plain sight. Look at the ceiling,'" Lily repeated.

"Yes!" Alex said, jumping into the air. "The cracked-plate clue that cracked the case!"

"The plate isn't cracked," AnaMaria pointed out.

"Oh," Alex admitted. "Well, it could still be the clue that cracks the case."

Lily was sure Alex was right. "We should go look at the ceilings at the old Winston house," she said. "And this afternoon we'll have the place to ourselves because Ms. O'Leary said she had to help at her granddaughter's Bible School, remember?"

On the way out, walking along in the June sunshine, Alex asked if any of them had seen signs of forced entry at either the old Winston place or the farm.

Since they hadn't, the girls started reviewing who had a house key.

"Well, Ms. O'Leary does, obviously," Elizabeth said.

"And we do," Alex added. "Duh."

"Annie said before she left that she'd given a key to Mr. Tuppin as her attorney," Lily reminded them.

"And Ms. O'Leary might have given her key to Les Dudley, since he's been coming and going so much," Kate said.

"And don't forget the spare key we found in the box on the back porch the very first day we went to the house," Lily reminded them. "Anybody could have found that."

"So in summary," Elizabeth said, "anybody in town could have a key."

Kate snapped the head off a black-eyed Susan growing beside the road and flung it at Elizabeth in disgust. "You should be ashamed," she said as the rest of the girls groaned at Elizabeth's old and awful pun about their town.

As they went through the front gates, which stood open, Lily stopped. "Now that we may be getting so close, we don't want to be surprised," she said. "How about half of us go in and compare the writing on the plate to the writing on the old newspaper? Then we'll look at ceilings. The other half can stand guard outside."

"OK," Kate said. "Why don't AnaMaria, Elizabeth, and I take guard duty?"

"Great!"

So Lily, Sarah, and Alex went inside, and, since Ms. O'Leary wasn't there, they decided to bring The White Rabbit down to help them hunt.

"Do him good to get out of that attic for a while," Sarah said, stroking the cat, who rubbed his chin against hers with a blissful rumble that made Sarah laugh.

Downstairs, the first thing they did was find the old newspaper clipping on which Dr. Winston had scribbled. When they held it up to the plate, the writing looked as if it had been done by the same person.

"Just as I expected," Lily said. "This plate is really a clue from Dr. Winston."

So they got to work looking at ceilings.

"Ah, it hurts," Sarah complained, rubbing her neck muscles after a while.

"Tell me," Alex agreed.

They had peered up at the ceilings in the foyer, the dining room, the living room, the sunroom, the kitchen, the butler's pantry, and the mudroom until Lily was dizzy. They saw nothing that was hidden in plain sight except the stray cobweb that Ms. O'Leary had missed.

"I'm going to lie down and look," Sarah announced as they went into the parlor.

So the girls lay on their backs and Lily made herself scrutinize every square inch of the ceiling. There was the crack that opened to reveal the secret door to the old vet's hidden office.

"Wait a minute!" she said, sitting up. "Wait a minute here …"

As if agreeing with her brilliance, The White Rabbit made a startled sound, leapt out of Sarah's arms, and raced off as if he were hunting something.

"What?" Sarah asked, propping herself up on an elbow.

"In the secret office—yes!" Lily was sure she was right. The ceilings in that room had been lowered.

"Follow me," she said, rushing to the molding and pulling it back to reveal the hidden door.

Inside, she pointed up. "Look."

"At what?" Alex asked.

"All the ceilings in the house are practically as high as heaven, right? And what do you notice about this one?"

"Not so high," Sarah said.

"Downright low," Alex agreed.

"So let's really look at this ceiling. As in really, really," Lily encouraged her friends.

"I saw a flashlight in the kitchen," Sarah said. "Ms. O or whoever won't mind if we borrow it."

She was off and back in seconds with the flashlight in her hand and The White Rabbit at her heels.

After playing the strong light carefully over the paneled ceiling, Lily finally saw it. A tiny latch in the corner. But still too high to reach.

So they rolled the vet's old wooden swivel chair over to the corner. Lily climbed up. The chair wobbled and turned despite Alex's and Sarah's efforts to hold it still.

Lily pushed against the latch and a section of the ceiling dropped from a concealed hinge. It came down with such ease and speed that she didn't have time to get out of the way. She toppled over, the swivel chair shooting out from under her, making Alex and Sarah scream as they tried to catch her. The White Rabbit howled and ran for cover.

"Man," Lily breathed, when the wind came back into her lungs, "would you look at that?"

"Ow, ow, ow!" Sarah moaned. "You're killing my leg!"

"Get off my fingers," Alex grumbled.

The girls helped each other up and hurried to look at the stairs that had dropped when Lily unfastened the latch.

Alex gave a low whistle, her hands on her hips. "Look what we found!"

"Stairs!" Lily clapped her hands and did a little dance. "C'mon!" she cried, leading the way. "Let's see!"

Her head spun with their success. They were near the old vet's treasure trove. She could *feel* it.

She flashed the light around just enough to tell that the space at the top of the stairs was mainly a cubbyhole with shelves crammed full of … pill bottles and medicine tins?

"What do you make of this?" she asked, giving Sarah and Alex a hand up.

"I dunno," Alex said.

"Yoo-hoo!" someone called.

It was Ms. O.

"Shhhhhhhh!" Lily said.

"Are you girls here?" Ms. O'Leary called, her voice growing fainter.

"Hurry," Lily said. "Leave the stairs down. We don't have time to put them up now. Let's get out of here and come back tonight when we can really explore."

Her legs were shaking so much she almost tumbled down the stairs. They were getting close!

She opened the old office's paneling just a crack and peered out into the parlor. She could hear Ms. O'Leary running water in the kitchen.

"C'mon," Lily hissed, waving to the girls. They eased out into the parlor.

Sarah whispered, "I'll take Rabbit back to the attic. Meet you outside."

Lily nodded, her fingers to her lips.

As she and Alex got closer to the kitchen, she called, "Ms. O'Leary? Is that you? We were just taking care of The White Rabbit."

"So early?" Ms. O'Leary asked, drying her hands.

"How was Bible School?" Lily asked.

"Oh." She seemed to be thinking. "Well, see, we didn't go. My little granddaughter—Cassie is her name. Did I ever tell you her name? Well, anyway, the urchin woke up this morning with a sore throat, so her mama called me. About nine it must have been—"

Ms. O'Leary was still explaining why she was there after all when Kate burst into the kitchen. "You'll never guess what we fou—" She stared at Ms. O'Leary.

Just then the doorbell rang.

After a long look at Kate, Ms. O'Leary went to see who it was. The girls stood frozen, listening. Finally, they heard Les Dudley's voice.

"Sorry, we didn't see her come in," Kate whispered. "We got sidetracked. Look what we found in the back garden."

Kate rolled the object between her fingers.

"A fountain pen," Alex said.

Kate nodded.

Lily nudged the girls toward the door. "Let's get out of here. Where we can talk."

Huddling by a crumbled statue of a naked lady, where nobody but the bushes could hear them, Kate explained what she and AnaMaria and Elizabeth had found.

"Actually, I found it," Elizabeth pointed out.

Kate shrugged. "But I had the idea of retracing Dracula's footsteps, assuming he'd hidden on the basement stairs that night until Lily and Sarah were out of the house, then followed them through the backyard to the gardener's gate."

"Good thinking!" Lily commended Kate.

"And guess what?" AnaMaria said. "There are initials on the pen."

"Initials?"

AnaMaria's smile told Lily that the initials would mean something. Lily turned the silver pen in the light. There, in elegant letters, were the initials *A. T.*

"Allan Terwho! Tex!"

"See!" AnaMaria said. "Remember? We wondered why he made such a big deal about us being the only people out at the farmhouse for ages and ages!"

Lily nodded. It made perfect sense.

Chapter 16

Later, Lily helped herself to a glass of milk and called her mother at work. She got permission to go to a slumber party at the carriage house. As she pondered the clues, she wondered if they might be jumping to conclusions.

Yes, most of the evidence pointed to Tex as the person they were racing against to find whatever the old vet had squirreled away. Tex had the right initials, he was a stranger in town, he drove a black pickup, and he seemed to know something about veterinary medicine.

But ... it was the "but" that troubled Lily.

But maybe they were jumping to conclusions.

For example, Snapper Tuppin was a lawyer. And weren't lawyers always guilty of something? And with a name like Snapper? Really. And who knew how much information about the old vet's affairs Mr. Tuppin had come by? After all, he was the trusted family lawyer.

And then there was Ms. O'Leary. Always around. Always sneaking up on people. Always whispering. Always wearing gloves, now that Lily thought of it. Was she up to something? Maybe she was in league with Les Dudley, who seemed to always be schlepping around the place with ladders and a flashlight.

And Les Dudley himself also drove a dark pickup—one that could have looked black that night Dracula nearly ran them down.

Lily rolled up her sleeping bag, stowed a flashlight, and raided the refrigerator for the dozen hot dogs she'd offered to contribute to their cookout at the carriage house.

The girls had decided they couldn't wait another day to explore the hidey hole. So they'd cook over the grill, stage a slumber party in the old carriage house, and slip out later. Then they would search the dim, jumbled space that Lily, Alex, and Sarah had gotten just a teasing peek of before Ms. O'Leary turned up.

Lily wanted to be prepared. For what, she wasn't sure. So she tucked in some old clothesline rope from the garage and some black face paint leftover from Halloween. And, as a final thought, she rolled up a black T-shirt and a dark knit cap in her sleeping bag.

Finally she fired off an e-mail to the Silly Stuff Club members before she left the house. "Operation Hidey Hole," she wrote. "Dark clothing recommended. I have face paint. Don't forget the marshmallows."

As Lily wheeled through town, her sleeping bag and a

small duffle strapped to her bike, she saw Les Dudley on Eli's patio. He was sipping something out of a tall glass.

"Yo," he said, nodding at her.

"How you doin'?" Lily said politely.

And a few blocks later, out by the pizza place, she saw Tex's truck parked diagonally at the curb. Tex was sitting in the cab and—of all people—Snapper Tuppin was leaning against the door. They were engaged in quiet conversation.

Tex saw Lily and made that little saluting gesture of his. "Howdy," he said.

Mr. Tuppin turned to look. He seemed startled to see Lily. "Evening," he mumbled.

"Good evening," Lily said, suspecting that she would see at least one of them later.

Chapter 17

It was after seven o'clock when the last member of the Silly Stuff Club showed up at Sarah's house. Sarah's dad had a charcoal fire going in the grill for them, and Lily laid out her hot dogs. Kate had brought buns, Alex two bags of chips, and AnaMaria some salsa that her mother had made. Elizabeth surprised them all with a creamy chocolate mousse.

"But you were going to bring marshmallows," Lily pointed out.

"It's our new housekeeper," Elizabeth explained. "She's wild about cooking. She had me grating chocolate until my fingertips were practically worn off."

"Tastes just like those little cups of chocolate pudding," Alex said, taking a bite and smacking her lips.

Elizabeth rolled her eyes. "Hardly." But she smiled.

The girls played badminton and rode their bikes up and

down Summary Lane, keeping their eyes open for any activity around the old Winston place.

It seemed to take forever for darkness to fall and for Sarah's family to settle in. But finally, when the only light came from the flickering fireflies, the girls changed into their black clothes and smeared their faces with face paint. Armed with flashlights and Lily's rope, they set off for the old Winston place.

"No lights unless we really, really need them," Lily cautioned. She remembered how she and Sarah had surprised Dracula because his light reflected off the trees.

A half-moon cast shadows on the floor of the foyer.

Sarah spoke softly. "Let's get The White Rabbit. He'll give us a warning if anybody is coming around."

The White Rabbit was delighted to see them, rubbing the side of his mouth against everybody's fingers.

In the parlor, by memory and moonlight, Lily swung back the paneling to reveal the hidden door to the old vet's office. And there, just as they had left them, were the drop-down stairs leading to the little hidey hole.

"Once we get up there, we can turn on our flashlights," Lily whispered, "because there aren't any windows. But I think somebody should stay down here as a lookout." She clipped one end of the thin rope to her belt loop. "The lookout will yank on this if anything suspicious happens down here. Volunteers?"

Lily wondered who would be brave enough to wait alone at the foot of the steps. And she wasn't surprised when Alex raised a finger.

"I'll do it," Alex whispered.

"Thanks," Lily whispered back.

Lily led the way, shining her light around the space as she felt the top of the stairs. She moved away to let the other girls go up.

They huddled in a very small area that looked to Lily to be maybe six feet by ten feet. She could stand upright, but she could easily touch the ceiling.

A single straight-back chair sat amidst dozens of tins of old veterinary medicines, and wooden crates overflowed with yet more tins.

AnaMaria picked up one and shone her flashlight on it. "Look at this," she murmured, reading the label. "'Glover's Imperial Digestive Pills for Dogs by Glover Company 119-121 Fifth Avenue, New York'! And here's another one. 'Phillip's Corona Ointment, Antiseptic Wound Ointment.'"

"There are zillions of them," Elizabeth breathed, sliding her light over the boxes. "The old guy sure didn't believe in throwing things away, did he?"

"We should take just one for our Silly Stuff collection," Lily whispered, picking up a tin of Digestive Pills for Dogs and shaking it.

She shook it again.

Shouldn't pills go *klunk, klunk, klunk*? Or *tink, tink, tink*?

"Hold a light on this," she told AnaMaria. And she opened the tin.

There were no digestive pills inside. Just bits of rolled-up paper—which came out into the light looking very green, even after all these years.

"Money!" AnaMaria breathed. "Look, everybody!"

Lily unfolded several bills. Tens and twenties. "There's a hundred dollars here!" she finally announced, trying to keep her voice low.

Yes! They had won! They had beat whoever to finding old Doc Winston's hidey hole and his rumored stash!

"Wow, will we have something to tell Annie when she gets back," Elizabeth whispered, reaching for her own tin of Digestive Pills. Inside were bills that also added up to a hundred dollars.

"Let me do one," Kate said, snatching a tin of Phillip's Corona Ointment.

"How much? How much?" Sarah asked, the flashlight shaking in her hand as she beamed it on Kate's find.

Kate counted for a long time. "Two hundred!" she said.

"Let's open another tin like that and see if it has two hundred again," Sarah suggested.

It did.

"So if there's two hundred dollars in every tin like that," Kate said, flashing her light on Sarah's tin, "and a hundred dollars in every tin like that," she said, flashing her light on Elizabeth's tin, "then there are thousands and thousands and thousands of dol—"

"Shh!" Lily hissed, feeling the tug on her belt loop. "Something's happening down below. Lights out!"

In the total darkness, Lily leaned toward her friends and whispered, "I'll go down. You all stay here and guard the money.

We found it. It's ours to give to Annie." And before they could say anything, she groped with her feet for the first step.

In seconds, coiling in the thin rope as she went, she stood with her arm touching Alex's. She put her lips right to Alex's ear. "What's happening?" she breathed.

Alex turned, putting her mouth to Lily's ear. Lily could more feel the words than hear them. She could also feel Alex trembling. "Dracula's back. He just passed down the hall headed toward the living room."

Well, if Dracula was still searching, he'd eventually end up back here. They had to put a stop to him. Unmask him. They couldn't go around the rest of their lives wondering who he—or she—was.

"He'll come in here," Lily breathed into Alex's ear. "We'll have the rope ready to trip him. We'll let him see the open hidden door. When he gets close to it, we'll all scream and turn on the lights. As he tries to run, you and I will raise the rope and *bam*! Down he goes!"

"Yeah. *Bam*. And then what?"

Lily bit her lip, her mind racing. Alex was right. And then what?

"Hey," Elizabeth whispered, materializing at their side. "I can kind of see in the dark when I get used to it. Cool!"

"Dracula's in the house," Lily told her in hushed tones. "Alex saw him go past the parlor door. He'll be back, though." And she whispered the plan to Elizabeth.

"And then what?" Elizabeth said.

"I don't know," Lily admitted.

"We need something to hit him with after he trips,"

Elizabeth murmured. "You can count on me."

She disappeared into the shadows before Lily could whisper, "No! Wait!"

But it was too late. Elizabeth was gone. So Lily and Alex took their stations on either side of the parlor door. Lily tied one end of the rope around the leg of a couch that probably weighed more than one of old Doc Winston's horses. She gave the other end to Alex.

Then as quickly as she could, without crashing into anything in the darkness, she made her way back up the steps into the hidey hole and told the other girls that they were going to bring down Dracula.

"When you see the light go on," she instructed them, "scream as loud as you can and run straight at him. He'll take off and trip over the rope, if we're lucky."

"And then what?" Kate said.

Lily shrugged in the darkness. "Elizabeth has some sort of plan."

"Oh," AnaMaria whispered. And even without being able to see her face, Lily sensed her doubt.

"Just do it, OK?"

"OK," the girls whispered.

"Where's The White Rabbit?" Lily asked.

"I dunno," Sarah said. "He wiggled out of my arms. He could be anyplace, I guess."

"Well …" Lily didn't know what to say. The plan was hers. She hoped it worked. Because if it didn't …

"Good luck," she whispered to her friends before she vanished back down the stairs.

"Good luck," she barely heard them whisper back.

She crossed the parlor and took up her station by the light switch. She waved to Alex, who was on the other side of the door, hunkered down. Somehow Alex saw her and waved back.

They waited.

Lily's ears ached with the strain of listening. How could a big old house be so totally silent? All she could hear was her own breathing—and her thudding heart, which she hoped no one else could hear.

But wait …

Maybe she could hear something else. A movement. And there, before she had time to think, stood a shrouded figure even darker than the darkness.

Lily clenched her teeth to keep from screaming. He—she—it was only inches away. But going farther away. Lily's pounding heart settled as Dracula moved toward the paneling that the girls had left open.

Maybe it was her imagination, but she thought she heard him make a noise of surprise. Or of satisfaction.

Now was the time to spring the trap. Before she lost her nerve, she pushed the light switch and the room exploded in a blaze of light. Something white, claws extended, screamed and dropped from the top of a massive china cupboard. A horde of black-clad, black-faced girls, shrieking and flailing their arms, charged out of the old vet's hidey hole.

The figure whirled and ran for the door, tripped exactly as Lily had predicted, and skidded into the hall.

"Having a bad night, are we, Mr. Tuppin?" Lily cried,

snatching back his hood and revealing his narrow fishy face. And in that instant, she recognized the smell she had caught out at the farm. The smell of cologne—sharp and gingery.

Snapper made as if to get up. Then he saw Elizabeth, her tongue protruding from one corner of her mouth, with an iron skillet cocked above her head. He settled back onto the floor.

Gathering his dignity as best he could, he looked around at the circle of girls. "Scared you, didn't I? I hope I taught you a lesson, messing around Ms. Winston's house in the middle of the night. Going out to her farm and using her key to go in and do who-knows-what. You girls should be home in bed."

"So should you, Mr. Tuppin," Lily said. "It's two in the morning."

"I've a mind to call the police," he said, glaring at the girls.

The White Rabbit growled, reducing Snapper's glare to a look of forced indignation.

"No, *we've* a mind to call the police," Lily said.

"Why? I've got a key that Ms. Winston gave me, along with permission to come on the premises." He dangled the key on a chain.

"Wearing that?" Alex said, pointing to his black shroud.

"Ms. Winston didn't specify a dress code," he said, his fishy eyes almost meeting in the middle of his narrow face. "You're fine ones to talk—with your painted faces."

"Well, we've got a key, too. And girls often wear makeup,

in case you hadn't noticed," Lily said, her patience running short. "And we're supposed to be here, taking care of The White Rabbit."

"That's not a rabbit," he said, looking at the bundle of fur Sarah now held in her arms and stroked, provoking a remarkably deep growl.

When the girls laughed, Mr. Tuppin seemed to give up.

"I guess I'll be on my way then," he said, getting to his knees. But he waited for Elizabeth to finally lower the skillet before he rose to his feet. When he got to the door he turned to face them, put his hands inside his cloak and raised it so that he looked just like a vampire.

"Bye-bye, girls," he snarled, and left.

"Yikes!" said Sarah. "I think now we know who Count Dracula was for sure."

"And I think we'll spend the night here, then," Lily said. "We're having a slumber party, though it's awfully hard to get any sleep around here."

The girls heard the sound of a vehicle start in the driveway and watched it turn onto Summary Lane. They hugged each other and shouted, doing a dance around the room. The White Rabbit arched his back and skittered about on his toes.

"Lily, how did you know it was Mr. Tuppin before you pulled back his hood?" Elizabeth wanted to know.

Lily giggled. "It was his big feet. Plus I had remembered hearing the guy working on the front gate call him Art one day. Then the three of you found the pen with the initials A. T. So it was a *snap*-per."

Elizabeth groaned. "And you bug *me* for making awful puns!"

And after reviewing their adventure in total detail, they agreed that no way could they go off and leave the cash fortune of the old vet unguarded. Then they settled down on the rug in the parlor to wait for morning.

Chapter 18

Lily started from her sleep when she heard the mansion's front door open and the noise of what sounded like suitcases or boxes being dropped on the foyer floor.

"Rabbit! Hello you old furry white thing," she heard Annie's voice say, followed by crooning and the famous growl.

Lily looked around sleepily. All the girls were sprawled on the rug outside the hidden door to the vet's old office.

They had fallen asleep toward dawn, finally coming down from the glorious adventure of finding the fortune and thwarting Snapper Tuppin.

"Yikes!" Sarah said, bolting upright. "I've got to get home! If my parents find out we're not sacked out in the carriage house, I'm toast!"

"Do I hear voices?" Annie called, coming down the hall.

"What—"

Lily could only imagine what they looked like with their black faces and black clothes and disheveled hair and the thin rope coiled neatly in the iron skillet beside Elizabeth.

Annie stared at everybody and everybody stared back.

"We can explain, Annie. Honestly," Lily began, but Annie was laughing so hard that she had to sit down in one of the stiff old parlor chairs and put her head in her hands until she could look at the girls with a sober face.

And then she noticed that the paneling was open, as was the door to the old vet's hidden office. "Ah," she said. "I see you've been exploring. It's good to have children in the house again! I was about your age when I found that piece of trick molding. My brother and I delighted in showing it to the occasional friend."

"So you knew it was there?" Sarah marveled.

"Of course," Annie said. "Not that there's anything in there. Heaven knows, we looked."

The girls exchanged sleepy glances. Maybe Annie hadn't looked far enough.

"I think we have something to show you," Lily said. "If you'd like to see."

Annie nodded. "I'd love to see. This old house might have a surprise or two in it yet." And she smiled in a way that said the girls weren't the only ones with secrets.

"Come on, then," Lily said, leading the way. "Kate, you can do the honors."

"*Voila!*" said Kate, presenting the stairs to Annie.

"Good grief!" Annie exclaimed, setting The White

Rabbit down. "How did you find those stairs?"

In a babble of voices, the girls told her about Dracula—who had turned out to be Snapper Tuppin—and the cellar, and the old farm, and Tex, and Ms. O'Leary, and Les Dudley, and the china plates, one with a clue on it. "And this is what we found last night in the nick of time," Lily said, opening a tin of Glover's Imperial Digestive Pills for Dogs. "These tins have a hundred dollars hidden in them! These," she said, opening a Phillip's Corona Ointment tin, "have two hundred dollars hidden in them!"

"Not that we personally opened them all," Kate clarified. "But assuming—"

"This is it!" Annie interrupted. "You girls found the money my granddad squirreled away! My brother and I always wondered if the old stories were true. But we never found this place! You girls are wonderful, you know that?"

Lily gazed at her friends. They were a scary-looking bunch at the moment, but she was glad Annie thought they were wonderful. Then she did a quick mental calculation based on a guess at the number of pill containers and the amount inside each. "Why, there must be seventy or eighty thousand dollars here!" she announced.

The look on Annie's face said this was great news. "Girls, you'll never guess where I've been—what I've been doing."

Annie was so full of surprises, Lily couldn't begin to guess.

"Well," Annie explained, "I've been on a buying trip. I'm going to turn this old place into the most fabulous crafts shop in Indiana. And you have no idea how much this money will help me start my new business!"

She looked around at the girls as if they had brought sunshine into her life. "In fact," she said, "would you like to help me unload some things I bought on my trip? And then I'll fix you breakfast."

Lily and her friends followed Annie out into the fresh morning. Annie handed Lily a box labeled "Glass Beads." The girls moved in single file and made several trips, carrying boxes of yarn, fasteners, paints, stencils, stamps, and crochet hooks.

"Just pile it in the foyer for now," Annie called.

When her SUV was unloaded, she asked the girls if they were done with the iron skillet. Lily took out her rope and handed the skillet to Annie, who headed for the kitchen.

Sarah called her parents and told them the girls were all at Annie's house taking care of The White Rabbit and would be back soon. Everybody scrubbed off the face paint.

Awhile later, as they finished their eggs and passed morsels of bacon to The White Rabbit, Lily asked Annie about Snapper Tuppin. "Why is he your lawyer? He seems a little … creepy."

Annie smiled. "*Was* my lawyer, thank you. I just called and gave him a piece of my mind. Fired him, too. But it's kind of sad," she admitted with a sigh. "See, my brother went to boarding school back East, and he was friends with Snapper's dad, Ware Tuppin. When they were boys, my brother brought Ware home with him on school holidays. In those days, we had a lot of fun sneaking around this old place, dodging my governess and the housekeeper and my grandmother. We found our grandfather's hidden office. And, of course, everybody had heard the rumors about the money stash. We looked for it, like kids do—"

She took a breath.

Lily thought Annie was beautiful with her pink and silver hair and the tiny white rabbit tattooed on her shoulder. But now she looked very sad.

"—but when my brother was killed in a boating accident at school, I lost contact with Ware, and I certainly didn't want to treasure hunt on my own anymore."

Lily nodded. She had heard that Annie's brother had been killed in a freak accident.

"I became a sort of wild child," Annie admitted. "I got my motorcycle, and the minute I was old enough, I split. And I've been gone all this time."

Annie stretched and yawned. "I'm getting too old to drive all night," she admitted.

"But what about Snapper Tuppin?" Lily reminded her.

"Well, when I came back a couple of weeks ago to open up this place, I was delighted to find a Tuppin practicing law here. And especially pleased that it was Ware's son. He was a little fishy," Annie mused. "I think he must have gotten that from his mother. His dad was very nice."

"I'll bet Snapper's dad told him about the house," Kate said. "Told him the stories of secret rooms and hidden treasure."

"Probably," Annie agreed. "And when I gave Snapper access to the house, I guess he couldn't resist looking for the money himself."

"But we found it first," AnaMaria said. "For you. For letting us put our silly stuff in your attic."

"Have you girls moved in a lot up there?" Annie asked.

"Just a few things," Alex said. "While we were taking care of Rabbit."

"We've been really busy with other stuff," Elizabeth pointed out.

"Indeed." Annie smiled. "Show me your stuff," she said. "I'd like to see what you very creative girls have been collecting."

They led her up to the attic and turned on the light over the rug that AnaMaria had chosen. In the circle of light, they'd arranged a few things. One was the red canvas shoe that had given Lily the bright idea about the old Winston place to begin with.

"Look," she said, handing the shoe to Annie.

Annie turned it over, reading the bottom, and then she laughed. "I know who wore this shoe!"

"Who?" Sarah asked.

Annie smiled. "Not telling."

"O-o-o-oh," the girls chorused.

"Do you think you could share this huge old attic with me?" Annie asked. "When I get my shop open, I want a place where people can actually come and do crafts if they want. And this space is cozy and perfect."

"It would be great to be up here with you," Lily said. "We might be thinking of getting rid of some of our silly stuff anyway."

She looked at the faces of her friends. They all nodded in agreement.

"But just some of it," AnaMaria amended. "Not all of it. Not the plates, for instance."

No, not the plates. They'd *never* get rid of the plates.

"'*Ha, ha, ha! He, he, he!*'" Elizabeth said.

"'*Parlez vous francaise? A oui oui!*'" Kate took up the chant.

Nobody, not even Kate, could remember the next line. But the plates would be part of their club forever. Too bad they never found the missing book, W through Z. Lily would bet it was still somewhere in Snapper Tuppin's office.

"I can't believe how inventive you girls were in finding my grandfather's money," Annie said.

"Maybe we should change the name of our club," Lily ventured, "if we're not going to have a lot of silly stuff anymore."

"To what?" Alex asked.

"How about The Creative Girls Club?" Annie suggested. "And you could have your meetings in Annie's Attic."

Lily could tell that her friends were as pleased as she was. They were still together, but this seemed new and exciting.

As they went back downstairs, Lily noticed that Annie still had the red shoe.

Ms. O'Leary was in the kitchen doing the dishes. She began telling Annie a long story about her little granddaughter's tonsils.

The girls were just getting ready to leave when the doorbell rang. It was Tex.

He frowned at the girls as they hovered behind Annie, but he raised his hat and gave Annie his business card. "I was just wondering if you had any interest in selling that farm out on the Old Wabash Road?" he finally asked, after explaining that he was a developer.

Annie tucked his card in her shirt pocket. "Thanks all the same, but I don't think so."

"Yes, ma'am," Tex said, loping down the stairs. "Call me if you happen to change your mind."

"Are you sure you don't want us to help you lug that stuff up to the attic before we leave?" Alex asked, pointing to the boxes they'd helped Annie unload earlier.

"With six of us, it would go fast," AnaMaria pointed out.

Annie accepted their offer, and the girls spent the next half-hour moving boxes of craft materials into Annie's Attic.

Ms. O'Leary offered them some lemonade before they left. As they sat on the back porch drinking it, they saw Les Dudley and Annie in the tumbledown garden. Les was red-faced and laughing as he turned over the red canvas shoe.

"'I love Melva Winston's hog,'" he read aloud, and then he and Annie put their arms around each other, still laughing.

The girls looked at each other. Honestly. Grown-ups.

But Annie was right, Lily knew. She and her friends were creative. How would they ever have brought down Dracula if she hadn't thought to bring the rope? How would they have solved the mystery without Kate's creative brain power? Each had contributed in her own way—not the least of which was Elizabeth and her skillet.

Chapter 19

That afternoon, Lily rocked in the porch swing, enjoying the rhythm of the creaking and cracking. How could life be so crazy for a few days, then suddenly become so calm?

Maybe she should get a pillow and a crafts magazine and curl up for a nice nap. She certainly hadn't gotten much sleep last night.

But life was getting back to normal now. Annie presided at the old Winston estate. Dr. Winston's hidden treasure rested in the right hands. Snapper Tuppin walked in shame.

Best of all, Sarah had called and said their family was not moving after all. Something had happened with her dad's job that was going to keep them right here in town.

In Summary, all was well.

Turn the page for a quick peek at the next book!
To read the entire first chapter of the second book,
as a sneak preview, just go to:

CreativeGirlsClub.com

And to find out how to get a FREE copy of the second
book, have an adult call:

(877) 226-5391 (this is a free call)

We'll send you a FREE copy of the second book in the
Creative Girls Club Mystery Book Series along with the third
book, which we'll send for a free 21-day review. If you decide
to keep the third book, you'll pay only $4.99, plus postage
and processing. You will then receive two more books in this
series every couple of months or so for as long as you wish,
always for just $4.99 each, plus postage and processing. You
can cancel at any time, with no obligation to buy even one
book. The second book of the series is yours to keep FREE in
any case.

These books are published by Annie's Attic, a leader in craft publishing
for more than 25 years. Your satisfaction is always fully guaranteed.

Mystery Series

Next in the

Mystery Series...

Cooking Up a Mystery

Lily was reading a crafts magazine in the porch swing when the phone rang. She ran to answer it.

"Our new housekeeper?" Elizabeth began. "The one who's the totally fab cook?"

"Yes …"

"Well, see, I don't know where she's gone! We were making Baked Alaska, the doorbell rang, she went to answer it, and she never came back!"

"Never came back?"

"Nope."

"How long ago?" Lily asked.

"Let's see. It was about twelve thirty. We were just starting to make the topping for the Baked Alaska. It's almost three now. She's been gone such a long time," Elizabeth said. "What do you suppose could have happened to her?"

"Gosh, Liz! I don't know, but I'll be right over!"